The Soliloquy of Sunni Ducayne

by

Terri McEachren-Levert

1979: The Tender Years

There is a loud crash – something thrown and broken. The voices are angry. I am 8 years old and I'm hiding under my bed, after being startled out of a deep sleep. My hands are cupped tightly over my ears, but no matter how hard I push into my head, I can hear every word, and I will memorize those words and replay them over and over again during many sleepless nights to come.

The first thing I heard was something about a paternity test.

"How long have you been hiding this?"

He tells her he has found the envelope with the results, unopened, hidden in her dresser, underneath all her clothes in the bottom drawer.

"It makes no never mind. Don't you trust me?" She is trying to sound outraged, but it comes out as timid and fearful.
In a booming voice, he says, "You've ruined any fragment of trust there ever was...", adding that he hasn't trusted her for a long time, and was putting two and two together. He was expecting the envelope and he went looking for it.

Envelope ripping...Silence...long silence...Then a deep sigh and a growl...then...chaos...

"Who is the father?! Who is it! You better damn well tell me now!"

"Give me that paper. Let me see."

"There's nothing to see. It's one hundred per cent not me. That's all you need to know. And I think you knew that all along. I think you were just hoping you wouldn't get caught. Well guess what? You're busted!"

More crashing and breaking...things are being thrown back and forth...dishes are being smashed, vases, nick knacks... things that meant something no longer mean anything.

Yelling and swearing and the most horrible things are coming out of both their mouths; words I'd never heard before. Name calling. Accusations. Blame.

It takes me a little bit to realize they are fighting over me. There are no other children to be the father, or not the father, of. Maybe he is just as mad at me. Maybe he thinks it's my fault too.

"How could you?! How dare you?!" His deep voice is

guttural and snarly. I've never heard it like that before and it scares me. The reality of the situation, the confirmation of the results, it all takes the breath out of him, and his voice trails off.

"Just calm down, there's no need to ..." Her voice sounds anxious and upset, but the rest of the sentence is lost during another loud crash.

The voices are getting closer to my room, as the argument rages on. I make myself as small as I can, deep underneath the bed, right in the upper corner against the wall. I wish I had my stuffed puppy under here with me to hang onto, but Mama got rid of all my stuffed animals awhile back. She called them unnecessary and junk, but they sure would make me feel better now. I have my little yellow blanket under the bed with me, pressed tight against my chest and held there with my arms. I can't let go of my ears....if I do, what is happening will get louder and be even more scary.

"How many years have you thrown away? Do you even know what you've done?! Do you have a clue how I feel right now?!"

He's so mad...he's turning into a monster. I know I wouldn't even recognize his face right now, if I saw it. I don't know this man. This is not my Daddy.

"Graham, stop yelling!" *S*he says, but she's yelling too. "Don't come near me! Stay away! We've had a lot of good years together since then...." Her voice trails off when his raises in anger again.

"It. Doesn't. Matter. How many more were there? How many Annie? Do you even know? Do you even care?"

The argument has reached my bedroom door. Their shadows in the doorway block the light coming into my room and now it's even darker. Just screaming shadows, that's all they are right now. I squeeze my eyes tight... don't even peek...

"Leave it be, leave me alone..."

"You need to get out. You need to get out of this house right now, and don't you even dare try to ..."

The argument is in my room. It is loud and raging. Something is tossed onto my bed and it bounces a bit, the squeaky springs getting caught up in my hair with the pressure. I hear a zipper, I hear drawers opening and then slamming shut. All the while, the yelling goes on and on. The yelling....the anger... it has spilled into the room and is slowly seeping around, covering every square inch. I feel sick. I feel something bad is going to happen; a dark foreboding that is going to follow me around for the rest of my life.

I try to tune out the voices, but I still catch bits of it. She has ceased being contrite and is now just as angry as him – matching him yell for yell, curse for curse.

Him: "Don't you dare take that child out of this house!"
Her: "She's mine and I'll damn well take her wherever I want!"
Him: "If you leave this house, you don't ever come back!"
Her: "I won't be! Get out of my way!"
Him: "You can't take her!"
Her: "You have no say! She's not yours!"

He has gone quiet in defeat. I hear him leave the room and kick the end table on the way by, sending the lamp smashing onto the wood floor. I open my fingers, and from under the bed, I can see his feet as he slumps heavily into his big easy chair. I used to sit on his lap in that chair and we would watch tv and read books. We would sing songs, he'd sing to me, or sing me to sleep. Most of all, we laughed a lot and we were happy....were..... now it's a place of sadness. I think he's crying.

Clatter, banging – she makes noises and is mumbling angry

words under her breath. She's saying bad things about him. That's not nice. I don't like that. I'm getting mad too, but it's not going to change anything; I have no say either.

A final zipper noise, then a suitcase lands on the floor in front of the bed. The blanket lifts up and her angry face is looking at me. She's saying something, telling me to come out. But I'm scared; I don't move. I keep my ears covered and close my eyes tight again. She curses and reaches under the bed and grabs a hold of my pyjama top. Her long, polished nails pierce into my skin, as she is yanking and pulling on me. I yank away and she curses a second time. She reaches in again and grabs my ankle and pulls hard. I try to kick and get away. I know I'm making her mad, but I'm suddenly so afraid of her. It won't be good if she gets me out from under the bed, it's going to be the start of something so bad...

She's too strong...she pulls hard and the back of my head hits the floor as I'm yanked out and plopped in the middle of the room. The safe darkness of underneath is replaced by harsh, angry brightness, as she flips on the light and looks around the room. She is making sure she has packed what she wanted and left the things she thinks should be left. She doesn't ask me what I want to put in the suitcase. I guess it doesn't matter. She already took away my stuffed puppy. I clutch my yellow blanket and pretend it's a puppy.

I am sniffling and crying and she has no time for that. She starts yelling at me to stop, just stop, just shut up...that makes him get off the chair and come bounding back over to the bedroom, but I'm scared of him too, I don't look up. I just sit there, whimpering. My eyes are too filled with tears to see anything anyway.

"It's not her fault. You leave her alone. You be nice to her!"

"Get out of my way, Graham!" She says, almost threateningly.

"Leave her here and just go... go away... just leave her here..." His authoritative voice turns into a plea.

"You will never see her or me again. Get up Sunni!"

I'm frozen, I can't move. I can only cry, but quietly so I don't upset anyone.

"I said, get up!" My arm is yanked and I'm pulled up and she is carrying me on her hip. She is pushing Daddy, pushing him away. I reach out to grab him and hold on, because I just know that if she takes me away, if she gets me out of the house...life will change forever.

I have his shirt in my hand and I hold on so tight and reach for him with the other hand. My blanket falls on the floor but I don't care, I need to hold on.

She rips my arm away from him easily and I'm forced to let go. I cry louder now, I scream. I want him to take me away from her, because suddenly she's scarier than his scariest voice.

He pleads with her to just let him hug me, just let him say goodbye...just one hug...but she's storming out the door. I grab for the door frame and squirm, trying to get out of her arms. The cold night air hits me with a strong punch, making me shiver through the thin material of my pyjamas. I wipe my eyes enough to see, and I look back over her shoulder at him.

He's so sad...he's crying...I've never seen him cry before, but he doesn't try to stop her. He lets her just walk out the door with me and the suitcases, and for that, I'll never forgive him.

It would be a long time before I ever had contact with him again, and an even longer time before we laid eyes on each other in person. Even when our relationship was repaired, I still never forgave him.

1979 to 1987: The Transient Years

I:

Middle of the night driving...my eyes are opening and closing...colours and lights flashing by. I'm half asleep, yet I can't sleep. If I do, I don't know what will happen. I won't know where I'm going to wake up. My cries have long since ebbed into quiet sobs and the occasional hiccup. I miss Daddy. I don't even know what happened...but eventually, later on, I would figure it out.

I'm in the front seat of Mama's big green car that Daddy always calls a "boat". She's driving and driving and not saying a word. She's driving angry, with lots of brake slamming, speeding up and slowing down. She's muttering under her breath, and doesn't even glance over at me. I'm bouncing around in the front without a seat belt, instead of being in my booster seat in the back. I try holding onto the seat, but the green velvet is slippery. Even at 8 years old, I'm too small and slight to travel in the front seat. I'm never supposed to be in the car without a seat belt on, so I try to pull it out and hook it together, but I'm not strong enough. The car is very bumpy and Mama doesn't help me, so I give up. I need my seat belt. I need other things too, but my needs are becoming an afterthought very quickly. I don't have my yellow blanket; it's still on the floor back home. Maybe he picked it up and put it back on my bed. Maybe he's holding it and still crying. Maybe I can get it when we go back home...but, as much as I hate to believe it, I have a feeling that I will never see home again.

My head sways and dips. It's so late. I'm so tired, but adrenaline is keeping me awake. The unknown is keeping me awake. The silence is keeping me awake. I wish she would say something, but at the same time, I never want to hear her speak again. She took me away from Daddy. I'm scared and sad and confused. My heart's been thumping since the yelling first woke me up.

I glance over at Mama driving with one hand, a shaky cigarette held between her fingers of the other. Her make up has streaked down her face, following a path of tears. She sniffs and wipes her eyes, smearing it worse.

I look away, back out the window. We have been driving for a long time. I don't dare ask where we are going. I don't dare ask anything or make a peep. Whatever happened involves me. I tore this family apart somehow, so I better be good. I better figure out quickly how to never be a bother ever again.

Just as I've fallen asleep, the car comes to a sudden stop in front of a little motel with a flashing neon sign. 'Sleep Nice Inn' flashes in bright neon colours. She doesn't say anything to me, but gets out of the car and slams the old, heavy door closed. I hold onto the bottom of the window with my fingertips and watch her go into the motel office. A few moments later, she comes out again with a key and moves the car in front of a room door. Number Six. I need to remember all these details, so I can tell Daddy where we are. She gets out again, grabs the suitcases, then comes around and opens my door. I look up at her, wondering if she is mad at me, then slip off the seat. She slams the door shut and then unlocks the room, opening the door wide. I walk in and stand there, not knowing what else to do. A musty smell wrinkles my nose, the dank room hasn't been used in awhile. She pushes past me and throws the suitcases on the floor beside the tv.

There are two double beds covered in green pattered bedspreads that match the thick green curtains. Mama crawls under the blankets of the bed closest to the bathroom, still in her clothes. She grunts at me to lay down and go to sleep and points at the other bed. I wish she would tell me something, talk to me, help me understand, but that would never be her way. This is the beginning of me being left to my own devices. It's scary and I need comforting, but I would adapt quickly, and I would make sure that I never needed comforting again.

I climb into the bed with my clothes on too. Pulling the blanket up over my head, I grab the second pillow and hug it tight, pretending it's my yellow blanket. When I finally fall into a fitful sleep, all I can dream about is Mama turning into a large, talon bird circling overhead as I'm running as fast as I can. Before I can get away, she swoops down, snatches me off the ground with her claws, and carries me away into the dark.

II:

The light wakes me up. She has pulled open the curtains, opened the door and stands in the doorway, smoking a cigarette.

I don't know what to expect, so I keep quiet. Sitting up, I watch as a lazy housefly flies in the open door, around the room and lands on the nightstand beside me. She's letting in the bugs.

"Well good morning, sweet girl." She looks over and greets me with a big smile on her face.

I'm confused. Is everything alright now? Are we going back home? I find my voice.

"Mama. Home?" I ask timidly, unable to speak more than two words. I'm not even sure if she hears me, because she ignores my question and starts speaking.

"My girl, it is a wonderful day. Do you know why?"

I shake my head.

"We are going on a wonderful adventure. Everything is brand new and exciting, and a million adventures await us." She sounds happy and wistful, looking up into the sky, as she speaks.

I'm still confused, but I don't dare ask any questions.

"We are going to discover new worlds, meet new people, travel, and live life however we want. Freedom. No rules, no routine, no one telling us how to behave and what to do. Doesn't that sound great?" She looks at me expectantly. I nod slightly, not want to ruin her good mood.

"Daddy?" It sneaks out before I even realize I've said it. I cover my mouth with my hand and look up at her in fear. What would she do if I reminded her of last night? Would she scream and yell? Hit me? Drive off and leave me here? Her behaviour has always been unpredictable, but now I am left to deal with it all by myself, and I don't know how.

"No more Daddy, sweet thing...Daddy is a thing of the past, not a thing of our future. He's not invited on our adventures. This is just you and me against the world, and we are going to find our way. Yes we will be just fine..." Her voice trails off sounding unsure, contradicting her brave words. Her cigarette burns down, the ashes almost touching her fingers. She smiles again, and flicks the cigarette butt into the parking lot.

I want to call him and tell him to find me and bring me home. I am coming to the understanding that I won't be seeing him again, and I am starting to mourn, even that fast. I miss him and his big bear hugs, and I miss spending the early hours of the morning with him, when Mama is still sleeping. That's our time, and I've never realized how special it actually is to me until I wake up here now, without him. When it's just him and I in the quiet, we sit out on the deck and watch the sun climbing the sky, listening to the birds. He drinks his coffee, and I drink my apple juice in a coffee mug. We talk quietly and he teaches me about the world around us; nature and animals and important things he thinks I should know. We talk about music; he explains how different instruments work, the meanings of various songs, and the hard work that goes into being a singer/songwriter. It's a business, he always says; it's not all fun and games.

Graham Sage is a rock star. That's what Mama always calls him. He's on the road a lot, travelling all over with his band, "Graham Sage and the Night Winds". His real full name is Graham Sage Ducayne, but his manager told him it sounded better to drop the Ducayne for a stage name. So Mama and I have his real last name, but he uses his middle name as a last name. I don't understand why he has to change his name so people will like his music better.

Daddy is away from home often, but then he comes home for long stretches of time. The more popular his music is becoming, not just locally, but world wide, the longer he is away. I feel like I'm competing with the rest of the world for his time and attention. When he is home, the house is filled with happiness and music; he is always playing guitar, singing, practising. Mama would shoo him and his band mates and friends down to the music room in the basement. I always sneak half way down the stairs and sit and listen to the music; taking in the smell of booze and smoke. Mama never comes looking for me. I sit for hours sometimes.

Alone with Mama, she rarely does anything maternal. She doesn't sing lullabies, or bandage scraped knees, or provide comfort after nightmares. It just isn't her way. She is generally pleasant enough to be around, but she has no desire to do anything involving child care or housework. I learned to take care of myself and not bother her. There is little supervision, next to no rules, and no routines. I do everything I need to take care of me. Somewhere deep inside, I know this isn't the way it's supposed to me, but it's just my normal. It's just life. I cope. I don't know any other way. Then when Daddy comes home, everything changes. He makes me lunches and suppers and tucks me in at night. He brings me places, he plays with me and most importantly he makes me feel safe. I need him in my life to balance what Mama lacks.

She has changed into a pretty white sundress with yellow flowers and strappy sandals. She decides that I need to be dressed in a similar happy, summery way, to celebrate our emancipation she says. She doesn't explain what that means, and I don't ask. It doesn't matter. It is whatever she wants now; all her way, all her decisions. I am inconsequential to her plans. I am merely a pretty little tow-along, and at the same time a terrible, terrible burden.

So I sit in the small bathtub while she washes my hair - she is not gentle, but I don't complain. Then I watch as she applies a new face of fresh make up; so much work to put all that stuff on her face. I would never wear a stitch of make up for the rest of my life. It was almost a passive aggressive rejection of anything she held dear. It was my only recourse really, but it became a lifelong aversion. Anti-mother, anti-Annie - that's what I would forever strive to be, and it was subconsciously decided right at that moment in the grungy motel room on the Missouri highway.

She gives me a towel to wrap around myself, and when I am out of the tub, she hums a happy tune as she dries and styles my hair. She puts it into pigtails with barrettes the colour of cherries. I sit silently, because she has never really attended to my hair or grooming before, so this is unusual. I don't know if I like it or not. I'm not used to being so close to her for such a period of time. She doesn't like to be hugged or touched much. She will permit it for a moment, but then pushes me away, usually with a smile. The intrusion of her personal space is an imposition she normally doesn't tolerate, even from her own child. I was never able to sit on her lap and cuddle; she wouldn't comfort me with a hug or smother me with kisses. She keeps me at arms length, like she does with everyone else. She is present in my life, yet she is absent. She's impossible to connect with, to feel close to. I don't bother trying anymore, I just accept her for who she is. I try not to take her rejection personally, because I don't think she means to act the way she does, but sometimes it does hurt. Sometimes I just need a Mama.

She picks out a sundress for me that's similar to hers, but

orange and white, and white sandals. When we are what she considers suitable, we are ready - but ready for what? I have no clue what to expect next. I don't like the unknown, nor the unnerving feeling that my whole world has shifted off kilter...but that feeling was to become a huge part of my life.

III:

The unrelenting sun beats down through the windshield and onto my face. Again, we are driving; seems like forever. Unable to get away from the heat, I'm uncomfortable and fidgety. The old car has no air conditioning. The windows are rolled down, but only hot air blows in. Mama doesn't seem to mind; cigarette between her fingers, one hand on the steering wheel, she sings along to the radio. The music is too loud.

"Where are we going?" I ask, unable to hide my annoyance and discomfort. I tug at the straps of my sundress which feel like they weigh a hundred pounds, and scratch my sweaty head.

She looks over at me, above her sunglasses, and takes her hand off the wheel to swat my hands away, "Leave it alone. You'll mess it all up."

The car lurches sideways and crosses the centre line.

Throwing her cigarette out the window, she grips the wheel with both hands, and pulls it back into the lane.

"I'm hungry and thirsty." I pout, unable to carry on the facade of obedience anymore, my discomfort getting the better of me.

"Give me a break, huh? We'll eat when we get there."

"Get where? Where are we going?" I whine. I am so hot, I just need to escape. I wish I could fly out the window.

"Sunni, children should be seen and not heard. Don't talk to me unless you are in a good mood." She cranks up the radio and keeps singing.

I sigh and lay down, curling up on the big bench-style front seat, not wearing a seat belt. Her reply was typical. I had heard it before. The only time Mama cares to interact with me is if I am happy and smiling and perfect. If I ever come to her with a problem, if I'm sick, or hurt or otherwise upset, I would be turned away and told to "come back when I had a smile on my face". I have heard that line so many times. Mama has no interest in wallowing in unhappiness with you, regardless of the cause. She doesn't want to be bothered by anything unpleasant, and she won't hear of anyone coming to her with their woes. I've learned to solve my own problems and deal with my own issues, and if I want attention from Mama or want to talk to her, it can only be about happy things. She always says that she "gets upset easily and doesn't wish to entertain such emotions". So I always confide in Daddy. Who will I confide in now? That thought sends a shiver of panic racing around inside me.

I must have fallen asleep, because the car is stopped and she's waking me up. I sit up slowly with my eyes half closed.

"Quick. Hurry up." She huffs with an exasperated sigh, trying to tidy my hair and fluff up my clothes.

She grabs my hand and pulls me out of the car. We are in a driveway of a trailer house, in a row of other houses that look pretty much the same. This one is beige and brown and nondescript. There is no grass in the yard, but lots of wind chimes hanging around – in the trees, on the porch – all with varying tones of melodic tinkling or annoying clanking. There are three cars parked around the yard, at least two of which have not worked in a long time; the hood wide up on one, and the front doors missing on another. A big black dog lays on the front porch, watching us with disinterest.

She's pulling me towards the door and it opens before we get there. A tall, thin lady steps out and rushes towards Mama. Her hair is coloured a dull red, and is teased and sprayed so high that it reminds me of the bouffants I've seen on the women in Mama's old movie magazines at home.

"Annie!" She squeals and hugs Mama. Her face has more make up on it than Mama's does, and when she leans in, the sickeningly strong scent of jasmine perfume makes me wrinkle my nose. She's tottering on high heels the colour of ripe tomatoes.

"Marva!" Mama exclaims, "we finally made it." She hugs her back, never letting go of my hand.

Marva looks down and says, "This must be Sunni. Nice to meet you honey. Oh that rhymes!" She smiles at me. I stare up at her as if I hadn't heard that rhyme a million times before. In fact, Daddy had written a song, just for me, with those words: "Sunni, honey, the sky's not blue without you...Sunni, honey, the ocean's don't roar when you're not near...Sunni, honey, the birds don't sing and the sun doesn't shine...Sunni, honey, I'm sure glad you're mine...". Sometimes I hear that song on the radio and it makes me smile, because that's my Daddy and that's my song. Suddenly I feel a strong lump of sadness settle into my throat and it feels like my heart has fallen out of my chest.

It was Daddy's idea to name me Sunni, I'm told, despite the fact that I was born with a head of silky hair the colour of coal dust. People expect someone named Sunni to be blonde, and Daddy liked the contradiction. Mama has blonde hair and blue eyes, so she was disappointed when I wasn't born to be her clone; my eyes are shiny green. She always says, 'Oh well, at least you weren't a boy', but I sense her disappointment that I don't resemble her. I don't resemble Daddy either, but now I know why.

Mama interrupts my thoughts, "Say hello, Sunni for Pete's sake. Sorry Marva, she just woke up"

We enter the trailer and there is a haze of cigarette smoke that can be seen in the sunbeams coming through the kitchen window. Mama lets go of my hand and joins Marva at the little two seat table beside the window. They talk for a moment and I stand there awkwardly, looking around. The trailer is small, crammed full of furniture, like there isn't enough room for all her stuff. Every square inch of the wall space seems to be covered in pictures, and posters, and decorations. There are nick knacks on every shelf, and rows and rows of books. I take it all in.

"Would you have something for the kid here? She's hungry.

We didn't eat before we left this morning." Mama says.

Marva jumps up, "Oh my goodness, you haven't eaten all day? It's nearly suppertime." Mama shrugs and says money is in short supply right now.

Just then my tummy rumbles, reminding me just how hungry I am.

Marva makes me a bologna sandwich with a glass of water, apologizing that she doesn't have much. She sets me up on the couch and turns on the little tv in front of me. I eat hungrily.

While I eat I hear them talking. Mama is saying that she "finally left him". She just couldn't "take it anymore". I don't think that she is explaining things right, and she says nothing about the fight or the fact that Daddy was so mad at her.

As soon as I'm done my sandwich, Mama shoos me outside. She wants to talk with Marva in private, no doubt to tell more lies. I go outside, but it is still so hot and there is nothing to do. I sit in the shade under the awning on the stairs and pet the lazy dog that is also too hot to move or care. I just sit there for a long time and the dog sits with me. Neither of us has anywhere to go.

IV:

Marva has set me up on a cot in the spare room to sleep. The suitcases are beside me. I have found a stuffed teddy bear on the shelf and Marva says I can play with it. There is a bed for Mama in here too, but she is busy in the other room, still talking to Marva. I lay there quietly, unable to sleep in this strange place. The blanket is itchy, and it doesn't smell like my room in here. The shadows are in different places, the door is in the wrong spot, the bed is facing the wrong way. I spend time counting all the differences between this room and my room. I can hear them talking and I listen really hard in case Mama tells Marva something that she won't tell me.

Mama asks if we can stay there awhile, just to catch our breath, until we find somewhere else to go. Marva says we are welcome to stay for a few days, but her place is small and she can't accommodate us for very long. Mama says just until she can get on her feet and try and get some money, maybe from Daddy. I perk up at the mention of Daddy. Maybe she'll change her mind and go home because she has no money, but I don't hear those words – those are the only words I want to hear...and she doesn't say them.

Marva and Mama are talking about high school days, and I

realize they have known each other for a long time, even though I've never heard of her before. Mama has never revealed too much about herself. I don't really even know her – she doesn't want to be known. She isn't close to anyone and keeps her secrets private. However, as I listen to their conversation late into the night, I learn a lot about Mama that I've never known before.

Marva laughs when she tells Mama that she, herself, never intended to live in a trailer park. She's sorry that Mama has to see her so downtrodden. She had hopes of better, but couldn't afford to go to college, got sidetracked by the wrong men, and her dreams faded away. So instead, she's a hairdresser, but she's not licensed, so she can only work for friends out of her home. It's not much of a living, she says, but giggles when she admits that alimony from two different husbands helps a bit, even if they were bums.

Mama surprises me when she shares that she had big plans back then also. She wanted to be a model or a movie star, and even made it to California briefly. She says she took a bus out there on a wing and prayer after high school and got a job as a waitress. She desperately wanted to be "discovered" and be able to leave her old, terrible life at home behind. Marva doesn't ask why life was terrible back then; maybe she already knows. Either way, Mama doesn't explain; she keeps that secret. She tried as long as she could in California, but the industry was cruel. She says it ate her up and spit her out. She ran into closed doors everywhere, constantly being told she was too young, or too old, or too skinny, or too fat, or too this or too that. She couldn't catch a break no matter what she did or how she re-invented herself over and over. She admits to Marva that she did some things she's not proud of for people that promised her a career – all for nothing. She never made it big. She never even made enough money to get a bus ticket ticket home; she had to call home and beg for that. Her heart was broken when she had to return home to her mother and her stepfather number four with her head hanging down. They wasted no time saying "I told you so", and laughed at her attempt to follow her dreams. The whole experience changed her, made her bitter, she says. She was desperately looking for a way out, but all she was left with was an eating disorder and the beginnings of a drug problem.

I hear Mama start to cry a bit. I've never heard or seen her cry before. Mama tends not to display much emotion, except annoyance. I see that one a lot. Mama explains to Marva that she became bitter and angry after California. She didn't care about anything anymore, and just went wild. She got into the local music scene and became a groupie. She would hang out after concerts, getting to know the bands that came into town and following them where she could. It was during this period, that she met Daddy. He played a show at her local concert hall; he was new on the scene and she was drawn to him instantly. She says Daddy was "one of the good ones". She realized she had found a good thing, and jumped at the chance to do everything she could to "land" him, so she would have someone to take care of her. When she realized he wouldn't give her the time of day if she was a strung out groupie, she straightened herself up fast.

Marva sighs then and says dreamily, "Ah, what a love story. He saved you from yourself."

Mama gives a little harrumph and a snort, "I don't know if I would call it love. It was need."

She further explains that she quickly lost herself in the relationship with Daddy. Her own hopes and dreams were quickly overshadowed by his fame. She was pushed into the background, as everyone was only interested in him. Everything was about him. She became resentful, but had nowhere else to go, and he was still a good man, so she stayed. Then she had a child, and there went the rest of her life. After I was born, she settled into a life of drudgery that she never expected when she had dreams of being a rock star's wife. The reality was disappointing. Motherhood was disappointing, so much so that she refused to experience it again. The feeling of being tied down was overwhelming. It became all about the baby, everyone fussed over the baby, and she lost herself again. She never recovered after giving birth, a quiet depression lingered.

I scowl, as I lay there hanging on every word, my head swimming with new information. She and Marva continue sharing the happenings of years gone by, and I ponder all secrets she's unknowingly shared with me. I've heard enough for now, I can't process anymore and I need to tune them out.

Mama doesn't have a lot of close friends, and it's clear she's enjoying her long lost friendship with Marva. People rarely come to our house to chat over a cup of coffee; but Mama does throw parties when Daddy isn't home that carry on loudly, long after I'm asleep. She also goes out a lot at night, often leaving me alone. Usually, she leaves after I am sleeping and comes back before I wake up. Sometimes I wake up during the night and find her gone. The first couple times, I was afraid; she never left a note and I had no idea where she was or how to reach her. There was nothing I could do, so I would go back to bed and she would be there in the morning when I woke up, usually sleeping for the better part of the day. I would make myself something to eat and entertain myself, waiting for her to wake up. I got used to being alone at night, and after awhile, it didn't scare me anymore. I welcomed the peace and slept soundly.

Over the next several days, I bide my time, waiting for something to happen. I know this isn't going to be our new life. Marva is starting to hint that we are overstaying our welcome. It has been more than a few days, and she asks Mama if she was able to get any money from Daddy. Mama said no, but I know that she hasn't even tried to call him. I want to call Daddy, but I don't dare try. I am never alone near the phone, and I'm not even sure if Daddy is home. Maybe he is on the road again. My heart aches that it might be a long time until I see him again.

I'm looking out the window on a day when the rain doesn't seem to want to stop. The little trailer is dull and gloomy; the small windows barely brighten the home in the sun, let alone on such a cloudy day. Mama and Marva are drinking coffee and talking at the little kitchen table. They must have forgotten that I'm nearby, or maybe they just don't care. Marva smooths the colourful flowered table cloth with her hand, and asks Mama why on earth she would leave without ensuring her financial security. They are married after all, she is entitled to money. Mama sighs heavily, revealing that she left that night in a rush, without any forethought. She smiles weakly, and admits to being stubborn and impulsive, that she always acts first and thinks later. Daddy has always insisted on handling all the money, she says; he doesn't trust her with his hard earned money. Not since he realized years ago that he was pulling in a good amount of money, but when he would return home from being on the road, the bank account would be nearly empty, with Mama being unable to explain why. She would spend his money as fast as he could make it. Suddenly she could afford everything she had been deprived of growing up, and she couldn't stop soothing herself by buying things. The bank accounts and credit cards are in his name. The only way she can access any money is to call him, and she refuses to do that. She doesn't want to talk to him again. She tries to sounds sure of herself, but she only ends up sounding like she's scared to contact him. Marva doesn't understand. She doesn't know why Mama actually left, so she doesn't know that Daddy has good reason to be mad at her. Nevertheless, Mama gets a little miffed when Marva suggests that Mama's poor planning will only end up in heartache for everyone.

I like Marva though, she's nice enough. She gives me cereal for breakfast, and something for supper. She finds a colouring book and crayons for me to occupy myself. She talks to me once in awhile. To fill the days, I play with the dog outside. Marva tells me he's an old lab named Jake, and he's way older than me, so he doesn't do much but lay around. He makes a good friend because doesn't run away when I whisper my secrets to him while I stroke his shiny black fur. He just sits quietly and listens, panting in the heat. Sometimes I go for walks and explore around the yard and nearby. I saw some older kids, but no one my age to play with. I'm used to being left to myself though, so I am fine. I just have to stay out of their way as much as I can. I'm hoping that Marva will try to convince Mama to go home, so I don't bother them and keep my fingers crossed.

I'm sitting outside on the steps one evening after a supper of canned pasta and bread. Mama comes out of the trailer and walks past me, going down the steps.

"Are we leaving Mama?" I stand up expectantly.

"No, I'm going out for awhile. You wait here. Marva will watch you. I'll see you later."

She doesn't say goodbye or give me a hug, but I don't expect her to. I watch her pull out of the driveway and drive off. I go inside and ask Marva where Mama is going. Marva says she's not sure, just that Mama wanted to go out for awhile. She doesn't seem upset or worried, so I settle down on the couch and watch tv beside her. I end up falling asleep, and Marva covers me with a blanket.

In the morning, I wake up and the trailer is quiet and I am alone in the living room. I look at the clock and it's 9 am. I get up and go into the spare room we've been staying in, expecting to see Mama sleeping after a night out. However, when I open the door, she's not there. The bed hasn't been slept in. Mama didn't come back. It makes no never mind – there's no rhyme or reason to what she does – she'll be back later. Maybe when she comes back, we can leave. Maybe we can go home. I will miss Marva though. I should probably pack my suitcase and get ready.

When Marva gets up awhile later, she is surprised to find Mama still not home. She gets on the phone and makes some calls. She paces whiles she talks, puffing on a cigarette. I watch tv and wait. My whole life is spent waiting.

When Mama still doesn't come back after another night, Marva contemplates calling the police. She is worried, but also getting annoyed. She says she's not a babysitter and how dare Mama take advantage. I feel like I'm in the way now and I hope Mama comes back soon.

Another night comes and goes. No Mama. Marva is getting fed up and angry. Not at me, but she's not thrilled that I'm hanging around. I try to make myself scarce and not eat too much of her food.

Finally, we hear the door open during the next night and Mama comes in. She's been gone 4 days. I am in bed, but I hear Marva rush out of her room to the door and ask Mama what on earth happened, where was she, what was wrong?

Mama mumbles vague apologies and says she needed to "get her head on straight" and find some money and a way to take care of us. She's met someone...

That's when Marva's concern is replaced by anger. She tells Mama that she needs to leave in the morning – she won't be taken advantage of. She can't afford to be a charity, and is not interested in being a babysitter.

They bicker back and forth. Mama gets angry too. She says no problem, we will get out of her hair right now. Marva says no, in the morning, let Sunni sleep...but Sunni is not sleeping. I am awake and my heart is pounding. Mama is mad, and I know she will have to prove a point and not wait until morning to leave. I'm about to be dragged out of bed; another middle of the night flight.

Sure enough, Marva follows Mama into the spare room, calmer now, trying to convince Mama to leave me sleep and they could discuss it all in the morning. But Mama is indignant and is determined to leave right away to show Marva that she will do what she wants. Again, suitcases are tossed onto the bed, as I sit there watching it all unfold, reminiscent of when she took me away from Daddy.

Mama shouts at me to get up and get my coat and get into the car. There is no time to say thank you and goodbye to Marva. It was pretty boring, but I liked her well enough. I hope she's not mad at me too. I want to make sure, but there is no time to talk to her – she is following Mama around the room trying to reason with her. I don't bother trying to get dressed, as Mama has thrown all my stuff into the suitcase anyway and then packs her own. I leave the two of them in the bedroom, still arguing, and go out and find my coat and put it on. Mama comes rushing out of the bedroom with the suitcases, opens the front door and marches to the car, without looking back. I am expected to follow without having to be told. I go to leave, but Marva stops me. I turn back and she hands me the teddy bear that I have been sleeping with. I thank her, hug her quickly and run out the door. I wonder how long it would be until Mama throws it away, calling it junk.

V:

We drive in silence, no radio, no cigarette – the only noise is the other cars whizzing past us going the opposite way. Her hands clench the wheel tightly, but she has the smallest hint of a smile on her lips.

I have no idea where we are going now. The car window is rolled down, and I smell the earthy, dark smells of the night as the winds blows my hair. I turn my head and look out into the blackness. Maybe we are going in the direction of home. I can't tell, but I can hope. I twirl my hair around my fingers anxiously, and settle back, preparing for another long ride. However, we don't drive very far, only a couple hours, even though I did see the sign that says we have now crossed over into Kentucky. The hope of going home vanishes; we are getting farther and farther away. Disappointment and despair settle over me.

We pull into the driveway of a little brick house. The house is not in good repair from what I can see in the darkness and moonlight. The grass is tall, and tickles the backs of my knees as I struggle to carry my suitcase and follow Mama towards the house. The front porch stairs are rickety and creaky. Mama knocks once and opens the door, yelling, "I'm back!"

I follow her inside timidly. The house is dimly lit and smells like smoke; unlike the milder scent of Marva's menthols, it's a rancid smell. The furniture is shabby and the kitchen is messy; dirty dishes sit on the table and fill the sink. But I'm delighted to see two cats laying on the floor, staring up at me quizzically – one is black and white, and one is pure black with the brightest green eyes, just like mine.

Suddenly a man comes around the corner, and I jump in surprise. He's very tall and has a beer belly and a beard; his flannel shirt open to reveal a t-shirt underneath. Towering over Mama, he scoops her up easily, and kisses her long and hard. She looks so small next to him. I try not to react, but I'm pretty upset and confused. I don't want to be here.

After he puts Mama down, she gestures to me and says, "This is my Sunni." She walks over to me and puts her hands on the back of my shoulders and pushes me forward a bit, as though presenting me. She strokes my hair. I look up at him, waiting to be judged.

He looks back at me, he hadn't noticed me. He is not pleased, I can see it in his eyes.

"You didn't say anything about no kid."

"I told you I was going to go get my baggage." Mama giggles at her own joke.

The man keeps a hard look on his face and stares at Mama.

"Oh come on now Ronnie. She's quiet as a mouse and won't be any trouble at all, will you Sunni?"

She glares down at me and I nod quickly. I don't want this big man to be mad at me, and I certainly don't feel welcome.

Ronnie grunts and picks up the suitcases and carries them into the other room. There is only one bedroom here, and I am not invited to sleep on a cot, or even on the floor. Instead I'm ushered to the shabby brown love seat which sits on the opposite wall of the matching couch. I'm given a blanket and told to go to sleep. Mama and Ronnie go into the bedroom and close the door. I look at the clock sitting on the end table with bright red numbers. It is 3:30 am. I'm too tired to process what is happening right now. I take off my coat, where I have been carrying the teddy bear, trying to keep it out of sight from Mama. Laying down, I cover myself with the blanket, clutching the teddy bear. Falling into a involuntary restless sleep, I can hear noises coming from the bedroom; noises I remember hearing at home when Daddy was away. I don't even care. I just miss Daddy, and I even miss Marva now.

When I wake up, the clock says 1:00 pm. The house is quiet. I can't believe I've slept so long. I am still carrying an exhaustion, but I don't think I can actually sleep anymore; I think it's in my mind. The stress of never knowing what is going to happen next or what to expect weighs heavily on me. Looking up at the curtain-less window above my love seat bed, I stare out at the sky long enough that I can see the clouds moving overhead. The black and white cat is laying by my feet. I forget to be scared for a moment, and carefully inch over to it, hoping it doesn't run away. It lays there and let's me pet it, and starts purring contentedly. I'm happy there are cats; maybe it won't be that bad here if Ronnie likes cats.

I'm still petting the cat, and the second one has joined us, when the bedroom door opens and Mama and Ronnie come out. Mama is only wearing a long t-shirt and Ronnie is only wearing jeans, no shirt or shoes. His big belly hangs out, and his belt isn't done up. I look away, uncomfortable. They have slept in too I guess.

I want to know what the cats' names are, but I'm afraid to speak. I just want to blend into the love seat so he doesn't notice me, doesn't look at me...but he does.

"Well you might as well come over here and have some food." He motions to me.

I go over and sit at the round table in the middle of the kitchen. He makes pancakes for everyone and I eat quietly, listening to Mama giggle and act silly and not like her usual self while talking to Ronnie. She's different around him, animated and expressive. Ronnie smiles once in awhile, but he's mostly quiet. When we're finished eating, I'm shown where the washroom is, and Mama tells me that they are going out for awhile, not to get into trouble, and not to open the door to anyone. They would be back later. They leave me alone, but I have the cats here so I will be okay.

I look around the house, being careful not to move or break anything. Ronnie's house is small and old; burgundy patterned wall paper is peeling off the wall in spots and the light brown carpet is dirty. There are no pictures on the walls, only a clock in the kitchen. Every so often, I catch a faint scent of something unpleasant that I can't place, perhaps just dirt and grime from years of needing a good cleaning. My clothes and hair feel dirty just from sleeping on the love seat, and I don't like that. I want to wash up, to wash this unfamiliar place off of me, but when I enter the bathroom, the bathtub is crusted in grime. So instead, I find a clean washcloth and do my best.

I don't know what I'm supposed to do now, so for awhile I just sit on the love seat, listening to the clock tick. I count the empty beer cans on the floor beside Ronnie's reclining chair, and look at the fishing magazine on the coffee table. There's a man and a little boy on the cover with big smiles on their faces, as they look at a small fish dangling from the boy's rod. Smiling, I remember Daddy taking me fishing once at the river down the road from our house. He laughed when the worms made me squeal, and told me about all the different kinds of fish there are, and showed me how to cast my line. When he caught one little fish, Daddy handed it to me, but it was slippery and slimy, and very quickly squirmed out of my hands. Daddy laughed and laughed. We threw the fish back in the water because Daddy said it needed it's Mama; he said all babies need their Mamas. I just looked at him blankly, because I didn't understand why.

Eventually, I run out of things to do, so I just sit and wait and play with the cats. I name the pure black one Blackie, and the black and white one, Sam. Mama and Ronnie don't come back until it's dark. I'm watching tv when they come in, hoping I don't get in trouble for turning it on. They are loud and stumbling, and Mama is still giggling. She throws a bag of take out food to me and I'm glad. The fridge only had beer and butter and ketchup in it, and I was getting really hungry. I gobble the burger and fries eagerly.

Ronnie goes into the bedroom and Mama comes and sits beside me on the love seat.

"I think we're going to stay here a little while. You'll like that won't you?" She smiles and there's a strong smell of booze on her breath.

"I want to go home Mama." I say bravely.

She stamps her foot on the ground and gets angry, her voice becoming a gruff growl. "This is not about what you want Sunni. I'm starting a new life and I'm doing what I want, I'm taking care of me. You are along for the ride." She takes a deep breath and simmers down a bit, "We are on an adventure Sunni. Enjoy the ride. Now be a good girl, don't cause me any trouble."

"Why can't I stay with Daddy?" I've never been so brave.

"Daddy doesn't exist anymore. Don't think about him, he's not real. There will be another daddy someday. Plus, Daddy doesn't want us around."

Those last words hurt my very soul. Was she telling the truth? He doesn't want me around? Another Daddy? I don't want another Daddy, especially not Ronnie. I want my own room, my own house and my own Daddy. She gets up without another word and joins Ronnie in the bedroom, closing the door with a bang. My lip starts to quiver and the tears fall before I can stop them. A curious cat jumps up and nuzzles my arm, and I bury my face in his fur. He stays with me as I sob myself to sleep.

For many years to come, I would wonder why she didn't just leave me with Daddy and go off on her own. She could have lived life the way she wanted, free of the responsibility of me. I will never know for sure, but I think she was driven by a strong sense of spite and vindictiveness, stubbornness and impulsivity. It certainly wasn't a sense of obligation or maternal instinct. Could there be any love involved? I like to think so, but I don't even know. Her motives and actions were a mystery to me when I was young, and our relationship would only get more complicated as I grew older. It would take me a lot of years to fully understand that everything she did was a reflection only of herself. None of it had anything to do with me. I was just caught in the cross-fire in her battle between her and her own demons.

We live in that little rundown house with Ronnie for what seems like an unbearably long time. Ronnie doesn't bother with me; he's not mean to me. He doesn't pay much attention to me at all. He mostly ignores me, and I'm okay with that. I stay out of his way. He doesn't say much, and is very quiet compared to Mama's constant chattering. He doesn't seem to go to work regularly. People bring their cars over to be fixed and he fixes them for cash. He gets some sort of cheque every month that he waits for and goes to the bank with right away, never letting Mama see or touch it.

I never get comfortable being here or sleeping on the love seat. It still feels like a temporary life. It feels like no life at all. Ronnie is irrelevant. He is a place to stay. I will never like him, even if he is the nicest man in the world. If I like Ronnie, then that will mean I accept him, and accept this life. It will mean that I'm rejecting Daddy. I vow that I will never let another man into my heart. If Mama stays with Ronnie, and wants me to call him Daddy, I won't do it. So I don't bother trying to connect with Ronnie at all. I keep distance between us. There is no need to bother with him; he is nothing to me. He is NOT my Daddy. I will not let Mama think for one second that I am alright with any of this.

Even with Ronnie and Mama around, I'm so lonely. The days are long. I spend a lot of time looking out the window; just waiting for something to happen. There are no other children around to play with, so I talk to the cats, and tell them my secrets and my wishes. I tell them all about Daddy, and when no one is around, I sing them the Sunni, Honey song. I have a notebook in which I write down my private thoughts, because if I don't get them out of my head, I will go crazy. I write exactly what I think about everything, and I fill it with bad words, fears and angry thoughts. As soon as I'm finished writing something, I tear it out of the book and rip it into a million little pieces so Mama will never, ever see it.

Ronnie and Mama have started to fight, yelling at each but often making up quickly, only to fight again. Mama has disappeared for a day or two a couple times, and Ronnie was so mad at her when she came back. While she was away, I would make myself vanish as best I could. He was upset the whole time she was gone, but not me, I knew she'd come back eventually. She always did, then she'd be extra nice to him for awhile, eventually taking off again.

Summer has ended and it's well into Autumn. The smell of wood smoke is in the air, and the leaves are bursting with yellow, red and orange. There is beauty around me, even in this dreary existence. If I can find something to appreciate and focus on when I'm feeling overwhelmed and hopeless, I can keep going. It becomes a coping mechanism, a way I can deal with the madness around me for a little while longer.

Mama thought about registering me for school, but she doesn't have any of the important papers needed to do it. She left important things at home with Daddy, and will not call him about it because she doesn't want him to know where we are. I think she is also worried that someone might be looking for us – or at least for me. It feels like we're hiding, and I just want someone to notice me, notice I'm here.

Once, I found a quarter on the ground and ran to the phone booth down the street. I put in the quarter and started to dial home. But I stopped before I got to the last number, before the operator came on to tell me I didn't have enough money to call another state long distance anyway. I stopped dialing because Mama's words came back to me in a rush: "He doesn't want us around." He probably doesn't want to hear from me. Maybe he's forgotten about me. I wouldn't try to call again, not for a long time. When I finally did call again years later, it would be out of sheer desperation.

Late October was my birthday. I had lost track of the days, let alone the month. Mama said happy birthday to me, and I had a little cake with 9 candles. Daddy always made sure he was home for my birthday. Even if he was away on tour, he would fly home, sometimes just for the day, to spend my birthday with me. We'd have a party with his friends and relatives that were close by, and some band mates and all their children. We'd dance and sing, and even Mama would enjoy the party. Mama had few relatives, and the ones she did have were far away. I don't know them, never visited them, never saw them at holidays. Half of my family, half of myself, was a mystery. It didn't bother me when we were all together, but alone with Mama, it was obvious that part of me was missing. I didn't realize for a long time that a part of her was missing too. She would often be surrounded by people, but none of then were hers. Hers were lost in a whirlwind of pain that she kept to herself.

The end of Ronnie comes unexpectedly one morning when the leaves have all turned brown and fallen off the trees. The overwhelming heat has been replaced by a constant chill in the air. Mama has gotten me a warm coat, a used one from the thrift shop nearby. I am outside stomping through a pile of crunchy leaves when she comes storming out of the house carrying the suitcases. Ronnie is following her, yelling. I run and hide behind a pile of old tires, unsure of what to do, my little heart racing.

I'm not sure what has happened between them, but I'm not surprised. I could feel the change coming. I knew it was only a matter of time. I also know that Mama is as fickle as the wind, and can change directions just as fast. She hollers my name, loud and angry, and I know that I need to get to that car really quick. I jump up and start running towards her. The tires are spinning, as she whips the car around and lays on the gas. She's driving away, kicking up a cloud of dirt and leaves.

"Mama! Mama wait! Wait! Stop!" I scream at the top of my lungs. I'm terrified that she will leave me here...take off without me...

I'm running as fast as my legs will carry me; my chest burning with breathlessness. It feels like I'm running forever, but it's only about 500 feet or so before she stops; the car lurches to a halt abruptly. Through the back window, I see her as she leans across the passenger's side and reaches for the door, swinging it wide open. I catch up and jump in, almost falling out again as she starts to drive before I can get the heavy door closed again.

Once we are driving away, I look back and see Ronnie standing in a cloud of dust stirred up by Mama's fast departure, and realize that I've left Marva's teddy bear in the house. That makes me sad. I will miss the cats, but I'm glad Mama stopped the car and let me in.

VI:

Mama doesn't seem to have a destination this time. She drives aimlessly, with the radio on low, the windows down, smoking one cigarette after another. She seems to be thinking really hard. Maybe she will decide to just go home, but I know too much time has passed and that is no longer an option.

I am lost in my thoughts and feeling sorry for myself, when

all of a sudden I hear it. I look over at Mama, she hasn't realized yet; she's too deep in thought. The radio is quiet, but I listen really hard and I smile when I hear, "Sunni, honey, the sky's not blue without you.... Sunni, honey, the ocean's don't roar when you're not near... Sunni, honey, the birds don't sing and the sun doesn't shine....." The radio is playing Daddy's song – my song! I've heard his music on the radio before of course, but this time is extra special. It makes tears fill my eyes, and I close them, soaking in the precious words, knowing Mama will soon take notice and probably turn it off. But she doesn't notice it, and I get all the way to the end and my face is wet with silent tears. She doesn't notice until the announcer comes on and his voice is louder than the music, saying, "That was Graham Sage and The Night Winds. That song is a few years old now, but Sunni, Honey is a classic we'll never tire of. Graham and the band are currently on the road, playing next in..." Click – Mama snaps off the radio abruptly. She glances over at me and huffs, telling me to wipe those tears off my face. It feels so good to hear Daddy's voice that I can't stop. I cry and sob, until I'm hiccuping and shaking. She yells at me to quit it, just stop it for Pete's sake.I turn towards the open window and let the wind rushing in dry my face. I look up at the sky and talk silently in my head to Daddy, willing him to come and find me.

The road goes on and on, and seems to last forever. There are long stretches of nothing, just straight dirt roads, lined with cornfields and dotted with small towns - most of which have few buildings, and don't even have stop lights. We have driven all day and the only thing I've had to eat is a chocolate bar and a soda that Mama picked up at the gas station. My stomach is rumbling something fierce. We are getting further and further from home. Mama has been quiet, not singing, not talking, not yelling. She has pulled into the parking lot of an all night diner and is parked in a quiet dark spot in the back of the lot, hidden by a row of transports. She turns off the car and it's so dark. I look at her questioningly. She reaches back and grabs an old blanket off the back seat and throws it over us, leaning back between the window and the seat uncomfortably.

"Aren't we going to a motel, or back to Marva's?" I ask. I would be so happy to at least go back to Marva's, but she might be mad that I lost the teddy bear.

"We don't have any damn money for a motel, and be damned if I'll ever set eyes on that Marva again. We don't need her. I just need time to think. Go to sleep and quit asking me questions." She closes her eyes.

It's cold and I want to snuggle into her for warmth, but I don't. Instead, I zip up my coat and pull up my hood, put on my mittens and curl up on the bench seat, making sure my feet don't touch Mama. My stomach continues to rumble, as I listen to Mama's quiet snoring.

The next morning, I wake up and I'm alone in the car. I don't know how long she's been gone. This time it makes me anxious. I can't stay alone in the car for days waiting for her to come back. I'm hungry and I have to go to the bathroom. I don't know what to do and I start to panic; my heart races. I get up on my knees on the seat and look out the windows, front and back, scanning the parking lot, trying to find her. I debate getting out of the car, but I'm scared. I've never been scared to be alone before, but this time I feel all alone in the world. My lip is quivering.

I wipe my eyes and look out the window again. I finally see Mama in a phone booth in front of the diner, and breath a sigh of relief. I've never been so happy to see her. I guess maybe I do love her a little bit. I need someone to take care of me, I can't do it all by myself.

She is talking on the phone for a long time and I keep my eye on her in case she doesn't come back to the car. But when she hangs up, she heads back my way with a smile on her face. She opens the door and looks in at me.

"Come on sweet sleepy head girl, we're going inside and we're going to have ourselves a nice restaurant breakfast. Mama's got a plan." She says in a sing song voice.

"I thought we don't have any money?" I slip off the seat and we walk across the parking lot towards the diner.

"We didn't have enough money for a motel, but now that I have a plan, we do have enough money to be able to eat."

We go inside and sit in a booth near the door. The seats are blue and white and spongy, and there is a long front counter with stools full of people. It smells so good; the aroma of bacon and eggs make my stomach almost nauseous with hunger pangs. Mama orders us both a big breakfast, and while we wait, she brings me into the washroom and helps me wash up a bit and waits while I do my business.

When the food finally arrives, I take a long drink of apple juice. I am so thirsty, I drink almost the whole glass. Mama gets us glasses of water, because they're free.

"What is your plan Mama?" I ask her, as I happily eat scrambled eggs and pancakes and toast. I need to eat as much as I can, because I don't know what is going to happen and I don't want to be hungry again for as long as possible.

"Well, I called your Uncle Freddie. I haven't talked to him in a long time, but he says we can come and stay with him. Isn't that great?" She smiles and drinks her coffee.

"I have an Uncle Freddie?" I ask, chewing and smacking my lips. I know so little about Mama and her family.

"Yes. He last saw you when you were a little thing, maybe 2 or 3, so you probably don't remember. He lives in Tennessee, so we are going on another long drive, but just one more time okay?"

I nod my head and keep eating. I'm happy to be going to see my Uncle. I'm happy Mama has a plan and I won't have to sleep in the car again tonight.

Mama and I are driving down the highway with the radio up loud and we are singing the songs at the top of our lungs. We are laughing and smiling and having such a good time. We are drinking soda and having burping contests. We laugh some more when I win. We count every red car we see and play "I Spy With My Little Eye". I like this Mama – I don't see her much. Sometimes it's like I have two Mama's, and usually the other Mama takes over and doesn't let this Mama come out much. I wish this was my only Mama. Good times with

Mama like this are few and far between. I'll cherish this time and hang on to it desperately in my memory, as it is one of the only times with her that I will feel anything akin to love.

The drive is long; but we have finally made it into Tennessee. I wonder how much farther we have to go, but I don't bother asking Mama. She's been quiet for the last little while. She's got one hand on the steering wheel and the other is holding a cigarette which she hasn't puffed on in awhile; it's long ashes are threatening to fall onto her lap. She looks wistfully out the window.

We are both tired, as we pull into the city where Uncle Freddie lives. The vast nothingness we've been driving through on the highways and back roads has given away to tall buildings and a lot of cars and people. It's very busy, and there is a lot to look at. Smells and sounds are everywhere; my senses are overwhelmed. We stop at a red light and I watch all the people cross in front of us. I haven't been in a big city before. I look way up and still can't see the tops of the skyscrapers. A bus drives by, cars are honking, men with construction vehicles are working on the side of the road. The smell from a hot dog cart on the sidewalk beside me comes wafting through my window.

It's after suppertime when Mama finally finds Uncle Freddie's house. It's been a long day. Mama told me he has a wife and 2 children, so I will have someone to play with – cousins! I'm so excited. This is the happiest I've been in a long time. I hope Mama doesn't do anything to ruin it. She pulls into the paved driveway; the big brick house is surrounded by a white picket fence. They come outside to greet us. I get out of the car with my suitcase and Mama runs to hug Uncle Freddie.

Uncle Freddie is a tall, slim, dark haired man with a moustache. He's handsome and well dressed in a striped dress shirt and dress pants. He looks the opposite of my short, blonde Mama in her grungy t-shirt and jeans with rips in the knee, but this is her brother. He hugs her tight, picking her up and spinning her around. The lady beside him, his wife, watches them, smiling.

"Oh Annie, it's been so long. You look exactly the same. I'm so glad you're here." He turns to the dark haired lady and says, "This is Kate, my wife. Kate, my sister Annie." Kate leans in and hugs Mama too, greeting her warmly.

Then they all turn to me. I set my suitcase on the ground and look up. Uncle Freddie is so tall, and so is Kate.

"This is my Sunni." Mama is smiling, she looks proud.

Uncle Freddie scoops me up and spins me around too. I giggle. He says, "Nice to see you again Sunni. I haven't seen you since you were just a little peanut. You've gotten so big and pretty." I smile and blush. He puts me down and Kate bends down to hug me too; her long, dark hair tickling my nose when she comes close. She is wearing a pretty gold necklace with a heart on it and sparkly earrings. I think she's beautiful.

They usher us into the house and Uncle Freddie carries the suitcases. Their house is so big, even bigger than our old house with Daddy. We sit on a couch beside a big picture window with fancy brown and gold curtains. The living room is big, and runs into an open kitchen/dining room. All the furniture is so fancy. It feels like a castle. I look around, taking it all in, and something in my heart knows that this is a good place to be.

Kate calls for the children to come and meet us. Estelle is 13 – she is Kate's daughter, but not Uncle Freddie's. I thought maybe this is similar to what happened with me and my Daddy, but no, it's just because she was born before Kate met Uncle Freddie; he's her stepfather. They are fine with this. I wish my Daddy would have been fine with me not being his, and not wanted us to leave. Or maybe he just wanted Mama to leave. I can't remember – parts of that night have become a hazy, traumatic blur. Evie is 6. She is Kate and Uncle Freddie's daughter. Both girls have long dark hair like their mother, like me. I feel like I fit in here. I think I could be happy. Oh please Mama, don't mess this up. Let me be happy for awhile.

Uncle Freddie is an accountant and Aunt Kate is a psychologist, who has an office in this house and sees her patients here on Monday, Tuesday, and Wednesday during the day, but only when the kids are at school. Kate tells Evie to bring me to the playroom just down the hall so we can play. Estelle is too old to play; she goes back to her own room. We sit down at a little plastic table and chairs to have a tea party. As I look around, in awe of all the toys, I keep one ear open so I can hear what Mama is saying.

She tells Uncle Freddie that she just had to leave Daddy because he was mean and hit us. I'm so mad - that's not true! Daddy would never hit anything! Until that night, I had never even heard him raise his voice. He was always calm and smiling. It took a lot to make him mad, that's why it was so scary when he finally did get good and mad. Daddy never did anything except love me. I wonder if he still does.

Kate and Uncle Freddie are sad for Mama and me. They say we are welcome to stay here as long as we need to. They will help us get on our feet, and even find our own place and a job for Mama if she wants to settle here. Mama has never had a job, so I can't imagine that. She is used to someone taking care of her, and doesn't really know how to take care of herself, let alone me. She goes on and on telling them how hard she has been working to take care of me on her own; that I am a handful, and she's tired and just needs a place to relax and get her bearings. It's been a hard, lonely year, she says. She promises them that we will be no trouble. She doesn't tell them about Ronnie, or that she keeps leaving me alone and disappearing, or that my Daddy isn't really my Daddy, and that's why we are in this mess in the first place. Mama blames nothing on herself and everything on Daddy. She lies smoothly and easily, and I won't forgive her for that.

Evie is fun to play with, even if she is a little younger than me. I haven't had a friend to play with in so long, so I forget about listening to Mama's lies and just enjoy the room full of toys. I need to just be me for awhile. I think we caught it just in time, before I totally lost me in the chaos.

Kate saved us some supper in case we hadn't eaten. We sit at their long wooden table on heavy wooden chairs, and I gobble up spaghetti and meatballs. It's so good. I haven't eaten real home cooked food in so long. Mama doesn't cook. She rarely even ate much at home. I just made myself whatever I could when Daddy wasn't home. I can even use one burner on the stove to warm up soup. I think I'm a good cook.

Uncle Freddie's house has lots of rooms and plenty of bedrooms. Estelle and Evie have their own rooms. Mama has a spare room all to herself. I can have a room of my own too, but Evie wants to me to stay in her room. She has bunk beds and I get the bottom bunk. I get to have a long bubble bath all to myself, and I wash my hair with pretty smelling shampoo. I haven't felt this clean, this normal, in a long time. I settle down to sleep under fresh smelling pink bed sheets and a thick pink comforter. For the first time in longer than I can even remember, I sleep with complete calm and no worries in my head. I sleep deeply and peacefully, dreaming of a future.

Mama and I settle in quickly. I even see Mama helping Kate with the cooking and doing dishes. They have a cleaning lady that comes in once a week to clean the house. I think they must be rich. Mama doesn't go off on her own much anymore, but has Kate or Uncle Freddie take her places she needs to go. Uncle Freddie tells Mama that I must go to school, that is non-negotiable if we are staying there. Mama explains she doesn't have any documents for me, that she had to run away in the middle of the night during "one of Daddy's fits of anger" and wasn't able to grab anything. Another lie. Uncle Freddie helps her get copies of things that she needs to register me in school. So for the first time in a long time, I am going to school!

I get on the bus every morning with Evie. Estelle gets on another bus and goes to a school for older kids. I make new friends and my teacher, Ms. Lansing, is so nice. She has pretty curly brown hair and bright red glasses, and wears dresses or skirts every day. She smiles a lot, and she never yells, even when kids aren't behaving. I feel comfortable and included here. The feeling of loneliness that I've been carrying for so long is finally gone. I consider confiding in Ms. Lansing about Mama and everything that's been happening, but I don't want to change her opinion of me. Right now, she thinks I'm just a normal kid, and that's all I want to be. I haven't felt normal in a long time. Plus, things at Uncle Freddie's are good and happy. Maybe I really can just be a normal kid here. Nobody needs to know anything. Besides, Mama whispered in my ear that I am not to talk about Daddy at school anyway.

Christmas comes and there is a huge Christmas tree and so many presents, even presents for me and Mama! There are new clothes for school, toys, and books. I'm so overwhelmed that I cry. Kate hugs me and says it's alright, I deserve it. Mama looks on and I can't read the expression on her face. She is a lot quieter lately than she ever has been before.

I meet new people, mostly Kate's relatives, over the holidays. Uncle Freddie and Mama have a Mama too, they mention her sometimes, but I can tell they don't like her and haven't seen her for a long time. They never mention their Daddy. I guess everyone has troubles with daddies.

I am part of a family now – my own, real family. I feel like Evie and Estelle are my sisters. I'm thriving, I'm happy. I still miss Daddy, and cry when I think about him too long. Sometimes late at night when everyone else is sleeping, I lay awake and think about him until the tears flow, and it feels good to get it out. I remember good times, like when we went to Sticks' wedding when I was smaller. Sticks is the long haired drummer in Daddy's band. He always gave me gum or candy when I would see him at the studio or when he came to our house to play music. At the wedding party, Daddy and I danced and danced all night. I stood on top of his feet and he held onto my hands, and we danced to the loud music all dressed up in our fancy clothes. He picked me up and swung me around and around, dancing under the colourful strobe lights in the darkened room. I think about going to the beach and Daddy teaching me how to swim, holding me in his arms in the water and telling me to kick, kick, kick my legs. I smile, remembering Daddy teaching me how to play the piano because my fingers were too small to play the guitar. He'd let me bang on the drums and he'd play his guitar, and we'd make up silly songs and we'd laugh and laugh. I smile as I cry.... it is a happy sad. Despite all the good things happening in my life right now, I'd give them all up in a heartbeat if I could have my Daddy back.

Months go by. Mama has not found a job. She stays in her room a lot and refuses to leave her bed for days at a time. I go to visit her in her room sometimes, and she alternates between shoo-ing me away and hugging me tight and begging me not to leave her. She seems to be overwhelmed and overshadowed by everything happening around her. She is not used to not being the centre of attention, of not being in control of everything, especially me. Kate is mothering me like her own kids – I think Mama might be getting jealous, even though she never wanted that role before. Uncle Freddie is starting to question her as to when she will find a job, and what she is doing to help herself and improve her situation. They never tell her she is no longer welcome, and for a long time, they had sympathy for her situation, especially given her supposed horrible circumstances. However, even I can tell that their patience is beginning to wear thin with her refusal to move forward.

The summer comes and goes. Things start to look up when Mama gets a part time job waitressing at a little restaurant.

She gets out of the house and makes a bit of money. Uncle Freddie and Kate are pleased...for awhile. Eventually though, they suspect Mama is telling them she is going to work, when she is actually going somewhere else. They don't accuse her, but I hear them whispering to each other about it. Sometimes Mama is gone overnight; still they don't say anything to her. She starts to do as she pleases, becoming less discreet, and she stops pretending to go to work in order to go out.

I worry that Uncle Freddie and Aunt Kate will be upset with me too, because of Mama's behaviour. I'm afraid that they will throw us out and we will be back in the old car driving and driving to nowhere. I worry about that constantly. I never want to go back to that life again. I wish Mama could just be better, do better, be a normal Mama; but it seems that's asking too much.

Many years later, I would be asked to describe Mama, to speak about her. It is hard to describe her in one word answers. The words flaky and flighty came to mind. I wanted to say she was non-nurturing, selfish, uncaring, had some sort of undiagnosed mental illness – definitely depression, possibly bi-polar - but that was not the time to reveal all of Mama's faults. It would not absolve or excuse Mama from her behaviour and from my upbringing – it would only make me seem bitter and unhealed. In the end, the only thing I could say that would do a service to both myself and my poor Mama was this: "Annie Ducayne was a free spirit, who didn't play by any rules. She blazed her own trail and took me along with her on her journey. She wasn't always the best equipped with the skills or means needed to take care of both of us, but she always maintained a fierce independence and was never satisfied with sitting still. She suffered from her own traumas in life that shaped her into the person that she became. In many ways, she was still that little girl searching for something to make her feel whole again". The rest of Mama's failings and foibles would be locked away in little box deep inside my heart, which only a select few would ever be privy too, and only after an extreme event forced it all out in the open.

VII:

My birthday comes and goes. I am 10 years old. Uncle Freddie and Aunt Kate give me a wonderful birthday party, just like Evie and Estelle have, with family and friends from school. There are games and presents and cake. Everyone has so much fun, especially me – the only one who isn't is Mama. She hangs back, standing alone in the corner of the yard with a drink in her hand, while Uncle Freddie keeps an eye on her as he barbecues. She has changed so much since she began living with her brother. I know now that she likely felt inadequate and ashamed. They say or do nothing to make her feel that way that I've ever heard, but maybe her own conscience was waking up and making her realize that there was more to life than always chasing something you would never be satisfied with.

Mama makes it all the way until the new year before she disappears in the night. We wake up one day in the dead of winter with Mama's room empty and her suitcase gone. She has left a note. Uncle Freddie doesn't let me read it, but I hear them re-reading to themselves incredulously later than night. Her note says she needs to focus on herself, and she is being lost in this pretentious house with 'holier than thou' people. She does not thank them for taking her in, rather, she vilifies them for trying to steal her child and trying to turn us both into something we're not. She apologizes sarcastically for not being good enough for them, and ends with, if they want Sunni so badly, they can have her.

Mama had kept it together for as long as she could. I think she had made an actual, honest attempt at the beginning to fit in and have a normal life, but she knew that she could never achieve it. It didn't feel right to her, and she couldn't hold up to what was expected of her. She needed to go, in order to feel like herself again. So now she is off and running, but this time, she doesn't take me with her. I am both relieved and offended; happy and sad; missing her and not caring at all. She'll be back. She always comes back. She has never fostered a connection between us, so I refuse to miss her too much.

I expect Mama to come back in a few days, maybe a week. When a week passes, I think for sure she'll come back in two weeks. The days pass with no word at all from Mama, no phone call. She has vanished into thin air. I'm not sure what is happening, but Uncle Freddie and Aunt Kate are concerned. They are sure she is fine, and they reassure me and themselves frequently, even though I do not ask. I'm sure she is fine too. She has just abandoned her burden on their doorstep.

Over a month has passed; life settles into a routine without Mama. I feel like Kate is my Mama now. Evie and Estelle are my sisters for real. We are so close – the three musketeers, Uncle calls us. I feel like a member of this family. and I'm ashamed to say that I don't miss Mama, not even a little bit. I wonder about her; wonder what she's doing and where she is. Just like I wonder about Daddy, but when I think about Mama I don't cry.

I still miss Daddy so much. My life is going by without him. He's missing so many things. I wonder if he thinks of me too.

He's probably lost in his music and has moved on with a new life. I hope he finds me one day. Would I even recognize him? Would he recognize me? Slowly another thought had started to creep into my head lately. Even though to me, he is my real Daddy, I know he's really not. So who is my real Daddy? I can't think about that too much. I convince myself I don't even care, because if I did, would it mean that I don't love my own Daddy anymore? I'm confused and torn, but I keep it all inside and just think about it myself. Mama has taught me never to bring my problems to others, and I never would. This will become so ingrained in me, that later in life, when I need someone to help me, I'd be unable to ask – until it's too late.

More and more weeks fly by without Mama. Uncle Freddie has hired someone to look for her, but she cannot be found. I wonder where she is hiding. Maybe she went back to Ronnie's or Marva's, but I don't offer my knowledge of where to look and they don't ask me. They start to discuss whether or not they should begin proceedings to get custody of me. I'm not sure what all that means, but if it means I can live here forever, then I hope they do. They talk about it a lot, and I so badly want to be a part of their family. I make sure that I'm well behaved, never get into trouble, and never fight with Evie or Estelle. I'm so happy to be somewhere where I'm wanted and loved so completely, that I don't dare do anything to ruin it.

In school I get good grades and I've become an avid reader, devouring book after book. Uncle Freddie says I can start taking lessons of some sort, I just have to choose what I would like to do – ballet, piano, sports – whatever interests me, he says. Of course, I choose music. I want to learn all the instruments and I want to sing. When I grow up, I want to be involved in music any way I can, so maybe one day, when I'm least expecting it, I will run into Daddy somewhere. If we do the same job, our paths might cross. I hold on to this and am determined to make it happen. I don't know any other way to find my way to Daddy. Mama has poisoned Uncle and Kate so badly against Daddy that they think he is a bad guy. They won't hear of me trying to contact him, let alone help me find him. I try to tell them that Mama has lied to them, that Daddy is not mean and I love him and miss him so much, but it's too late. The damage is done.

Months have gone by. Even I'm starting to think that Mama might not come back this time. She's never been gone this long. I guess she just got tired of being a Mama for good. Aunt Kate asks me every once in awhile if I'm alright, if I'm sad, if I miss Mama. I tell her I'm fine, but she doesn't seem to believe me. I hear her tell Uncle Freddie that I'm resilient, but she's still worried that I will bottle everything up and self destruct some day. I don't understand what that means. I'm 11 now, and I think I'm just fine.

Uncle Freddie begins proceedings to get custody of me. Papers are drawn up and it's winding it's way through the courts. However, it is a very slow process, as a real attempt has to be made to find Mama, as she still has rights, he tells me. I'm afraid of them finding her; I'm afraid of them not finding her. Uncle and Kate talk about adopting me and I would like that very much. I want Kate to be my Mama for real. I've always wanted a Mama just like her. All those lonely nights that I wished and prayed for a Mama like Kate, and it's now come true. I feel so lucky. Maybe my story will finally have a happy ending.

I could go on and on about life with Uncle Freddie and Aunt Kate, but it would be all for nothing. The simple fact is, Mama came back. A lot of time had passed, but she came back. She showed up, out of the blue, unexpected, and unwelcome. She turned my world upside down again.

One evening in the spring, we are all in the living room watching a movie. Kate, Evie, Estelle and I share a big blanket on the couch, all huddled together. There is a knock on the door and when Kate answers it, Mama strolls in, as though she never left, a big man at her side. Over a year had passed, yet she looked exactly the same, maybe a little rougher around the edges. She has a hard look on her face and I know she means business.

"Annie, what on earth..." Uncle Freddie gets up and strides over to her angrily.

"I've come to collect my Sunni. Thank you for watching her, but I'm going to take her with me now." Mama says calmly.

Kate gathers us girls around her, hanging onto me particularly tight.

Uncle says that's not going to happen. The big man beside Mama eyes him, expecting trouble. He is stocky and bald, with a big handlebar moustache. He has a mean face; he's scary looking. I can see tattoos on the backs of both his hands.

Mama sighs heavily, leans against the wall, and tells Uncle that she hasn't come here to fight. She calls over to me to go pack a bag. I look up at Kate and she shakes her head at me, so I don't move, frozen to the spot. She encircles me in her arms and I hide my face in her shirt, peeking out at Mama.

Uncle threatens to call the police. His hands are on his hips, and his voice is strong and authoritative. Mama says she appreciates all he's done for us, she really does, but then she gets angry and says she got word that they were trying to find her because they were "trying to steal my Sunni away" and she won't let that happen.

Uncle Freddie interrupts her with an angry growl, "You abandoned this child, Annie!"

Mama says she did not, and she will not give up her rights. She shouts at me, sounding angry this time, to come to her.

Again, I don't move. She's just a stranger now.

The argument between Mama and Uncle rages on. Kate is in a shocked silence, but has managed to grab the phone and is holding the receiver, ready to dial. Evie pulls the big blanket over her face and Estelle's mouth is agape. The bald man continues to say nothing, just standing there menacingly, in silent support of Mama. They yell back and forth and it's like I'm on the ceiling watching it all unfold. Uncle Freddie is not going to win this argument. Eventually Mama has enough of words and nods to the bald man. He pulls a gun out of the back waistband of his jeans and everything starts to become a frightening blur, like it's happening in slow motion. Kate drops the phone in surprise. It crashes to the floor with a loud bang, the dinging echoes in my head. I can't even tell what happens next because my eyes are closed and I'm covering my ears. I'm right back under that bed at home, hiding while Mama and Daddy fight. I know that Mama went into my bedroom and filled a suitcase with my clothes. The man comes over and wrestles me out of Kate's grasp, and carries me like a football out to the door. I'm screaming and crying and kicking. I'm being thrown into a car. I hear Uncle yelling that he's calling the police and they won't get far. He yells to me that they will find me.

And just like that, I'm gone.

Just like that, I'm back in Mama's world. It's like the whole past year never happened, like it was all a dream and I've now woken up back where I was before. As the small, cramped sports car is speeding down the road, I keep looking out the back window, waiting and expecting to see Uncle's car or police cars coming after me. But there is no one following us. Mama is in the front seat, hooting and hollering over her success. She is talking to me, but I can't hear her. My biggest fear has just come true. I can't cry, I'm all cried out. I just sit there in stunned silence.

VIII:

Mama does not try to comfort me. She is more interested in the fact that she has accomplished what she set out to do. She is proud of herself; high-fiving the man with the gun. He smirks, but doesn't say too much, listening to her excited chatter. What she does do, mercifully, is leave me alone while I sleep a nightmarish sleep in the backseat of that car.

I don't know how long we drove or how long I slept. I wake up to find that we have driven out of town and have turned off the main road onto a long bush road, leading to a long gravel driveway. The moon is full and bright as we are pulling into a dusty field, with several small houses spread out on the property, all contained by wooden fencing around the perimeter. It looks like a farm, but there are no barn or animals to be seen. It's more like a compound, and there are several motor bikes and a couple cars and trucks parked in various places around the yard. It is lonely and isolated here. A strong, uneasy feeling settles over me.

Mama takes my suitcase in one hand and opens the car door with the other, pulling me out of the car. The man has gotten out and is leading us to the larger, wooden ramshackle house in the middle of the yard.

I find my voice. I did not want to be here. This is not where I belong. This is not the life I want. I stop walking and jerk my hand away from hers.

"Mama! Bring me back to Uncle Freddie's!" I demand with as much strength as I could muster.

I am a bit fearful of how she'll react, but I am so mad. The time spent away from Mama had provided me with some much need confidence and self-esteem, but only a little bit. She still has the ability to easily intimidate me, and I back right down when she turns to glare at me. She stops walking and gets down on one knee in front of me. I am unsure what is going to happen, so I brace myself in case a hand flies at me.

"Sunni, you're supposed to be with your Mama. I came back to rescue you, so we could be together. I missed you so much." She says calmly, gathering me into her arms in a tight, squishy hug.

I squirm and pull away.

"No Mama! I don't want to be here. Bring me back!" I implore, my voice losing it's strength, and ends up as a whine.

She ignores my pleading, "Come on, I want you to meet my friends."

The man at the door is holding it open, waiting for us. We step in and a loud, booming voice greets us. I'm startled, and begin to shake in fear.

"Well it's about time you came back. We've been waiting." A man with a bushy dark beard and moustache gets up from the kitchen table and walks towards us. I hide slightly behind Mama. The man is wearing a white tank top; he's muscular, with multiple tattoos. His chest, arms and even the knuckles of his hands are covered in tattoos big and small. He is a nice looking man; he looks like he should be friendly, but his smile is not nice. It is an evil smile, and I don't like him at once.

I look around and there are several faces looking back at me. A scruffy looking man is sitting on an equally scruffy looking brown patterned couch, with a cigarette hanging out of his mouth and a beer in one hand. There is a woman sitting on either side of him. On the left, a woman with long blonde hair with a face full of make up, wearing a short skirt; on the right, the other has shorter dark hair, and wears jean shorts and a t shirt. Multiple tattoos cover them also. The man even has a tattoos on his face and neck, a large skull peaks above the collar of his shirt. At the kitchen table sits two more men, wearing leather vests with patches on them over t-shirts. The bearded man greets Mama with hug and a kiss on her forehead. She melts into him happily, before turning to me and introducing me.

"Well Sunni," he says squatting down at my level, "I'm glad you came to join our family." He tweaks my cheek playfully and I pull away. His eyes flicker with anger ever so slightly, but he recovers with a smile and stands back up.

I don't want to be a part of this family! I want to be back in the bottom bunk of Evie's room, listening to Kate read her a bedtime story. Then Uncle Freddie will come in and they will both kiss us goodnight and he'll say, "Good night, sleep tight, don't let the bed bugs bite" before leaving the room, and leaving the door slightly open with the hall light shining in. That is where I feel safe and loved. I'm so mad at Mama. Why couldn't she just leave me alone?

They are probably looking for me – they will be here any moment with the police to take me back. They'll take Mama to jail and then I can be free. Uncle Freddie said they would find me, and I have to believe that. But I wonder if Mama has found a place to hide that's so good that we will never be found. How will I ever get out of this mess? I've never felt so hopeless. Is someone going to find me, or do I just have to accept that I can't escape my fate? Maybe I'm just destined to always be stuck with her, linked with her, wherever her story takes her. I want to live my own story.

I see guns and even some money on kitchen table; and on the

coffee table, more guns, empty liquor bottles, and lines of white powder. The bearded man thanks the bald man and hands him some money. The bald man leaves the house and I hear the rumble of a motorcycle, as he drives off, leaving his sports car parked in the yard. I look out the window; watching the lights of his bike fade away in the darkness. I keep waiting for the flashing lights of police cars to be seen in the distance getting closer and closer, but the night is still and black.

I have a room to sleep here. It is a very small room that used to be a large closet. They have put a mattress on the floor inside, along with a lamp and a small table. This is where I'm supposed to sleep - a far cry from the luxury at Uncle Freddie's. At least they don't expect me to sleep on the couch, that would be worse. My new room has no window; I can't even look at the sky and talk to Daddy, so I try to send him messages with my mind. I feel all alone in the world. I look through my suitcase full of clothes and realize that once again, Mama didn't bring any of my stuffed animals. She thinks they are junk.

I have no tears left to cry. I might never cry again. In fact, for the rest of my life, there is nothing that really makes me cry – not even when it would be a normal, expected response. I've had to build a brick wall around me to cope with this life, and that wall is thick and strong. It protects me from everyone else, as well as from my own feelings. I don't feel anything anymore. It's the only way a little girl can process the madness around her. It would be a long time before anyone was able to wake up my sleeping heart again. I think my soul has been killed.

I find out that Mama's bearded, tattooed boyfriend's name is Shawn but they call him Stark. I am never, ever to call him Shawn, it would make him mad - he hates that name. Everyone seems to have a nickname, which is also sewn on their vests. I stay quiet, and I listen and absorb everything. I might need to be able to recall these details one day, so it's important that I know everything I can. The bald man who had the gun – his name is Krane. He is trusted more than anyone else, and seems to do whatever he is ordered to do. Stark says that Krane fixes things, and he laughs when he says this. I don't ever see Krane carrying any tools, so I guess that's not the kind of fixer he is.

Mama is never far from Stark's side. She tells me that they are part of a bigger motorcycle club, and never to call it a gang, they don't like that. She tells me she met him at a bar in the neighbouring town, and quickly moved in with him to be his "old lady". I know that she was looking for somewhere to go, and this whole situation is likely due to necessity and survival. Mama didn't want to be lonely and sleep in her car either, but I can't see how this would be better. I'd rather be in the car than with these scary people. I feel sorry for Mama, but I'm too angry to feel any real empathy. My heart hardens even more when Mama starts taking pills that Stark gives her in an unmarked pill bottle. I don't know what they are, but when she takes them, she zones out for awhile or sleeps for a long time. Mama says they calm her nerves and make her fly.

Over the years, even before we left Daddy, my anger at Mama was slowly growing and boiling. I have so much anger in me, I feel it inside my very being- just sitting there like a big, black lump in my chest. I ignore it and never let it see the light of day. I have locked it away, in a box deep inside my heart and I have thrown away the key. I'm afraid that if, and when, I ever unlock that box, chaos will happen. I don't know who I will become if all my traumas and fears and disappointments don't stay hidden where I can I control them. This is how I cope with this crazy life. This is not my life, this is Mama's life.

Stark has a bad temper. He is always yelling and throwing things. He yells at me for no reason, and is always complaining to Mama about me, no matter how small and quiet I try to make myself. I learn to hide really fast to stay out of his way, and make sure that I am seen and not heard. He and Mama are always fighting - not the way she argued with Ronnie – that was nothing compared to this. Stark is mean. When he yells, it is unlike anything I've heard before. He roars and his eyes change. His face contorts and turns red. Even when he is not angry, he seems to always be on the verge of exploding. He is wound up so tight, any little thing will set him off. There is something very wrong with him and I am scared of him....and I am scared for Mama. I think Mama is scared too, but she escapes into her pill bottle when it all gets too much for her. I have no way to escape; I'm stuck living every moment of this miserable life. I found her bottle on the table once. I opened it up and poured the few that were left into my hand, letting them roll around in my palm. For a very brief moment, I thought about taking one of the little pills so I could escape too. I even thought about taking all of them; the ultimate escape. In the end, I poured them into the sink, turned the water on and washed them away. Something inside me keeps me fighting.

Days and weeks are passing and no one is coming for me. I guess they can't find me, and I have no way to let them know that I'm here. I don't even know where "here" is. I could be in a different state, I could be a few miles or a few hours away from Uncle Freddie. I am disoriented and unsettled. I spend a lot of my time outside, walking as far up the long dirt road as I can before Mama calls me back. I figure if I can just get further and further, someone will see me. If I can just get to the main road, I have a chance at being found, but the driveway goes on forever, and I never make it past the big maple tree, which is 453 steps away from the house, before Mama notices I'm gone.

The other men and women I met the first night, all live here also, in other buildings in the compound. The man that was on the couch, his name is Brewster, but they call him Brew. He looks at me funny, and it makes my skin crawl and the hairs stand up on the back of my neck. I make sure never to be alone with him. I hide when I need to. One time, I didn't hide fast enough, but I can't remember anything else about that. When I try to remember, everything just goes black. So I find better places to hide. Living with Mama has made my intuition well developed, and I trust it. I know immediately who is good and who is bad. At least I know that whatever happens, I can always trust myself. I depend and rely on myself, and that is how I'm surviving.

The women are named Tru and Molly. Molly is Brew's girlfriend; she had blonde hair when I first saw her, but it seems to be a different colour every other week. She doesn't pay much attention to me; sometimes she rolls her eyes and seems annoyed that I'm around. One time, she cornered me and told me she better never catch me looking at Brew. She must have noticed the way he looks at me. I wish she would tell him to stop. She seems almost jealous, and she doesn't like me being here. I don't like her either, so I stay away from her. I tried to tell Mama about her, and about Brew, but she shushed me right away. She doesn't want to hear it, so I don't try again.

Tru, on the other hand, is nicer. She is the one with short dark hair, and wears earrings the size of wind chimes. She polishes my nails with pretty pink polish, while she hums or sings. She lets me wear some of her jewellery, like her clip on earrings and large, colourful necklaces. When we're alone, she tells me she always wanted to have a daughter, but she can't have one. I like her best; even better than Mama. Her boyfriend is Gray, the other member of the group, called that for his prematurely coloured hair - he's also nice to me. I'm not afraid of either of them.

During the days, the men are frequently away. I don't think they actually have real jobs, but somehow they always have enough money. Sometimes people come to the main house where Mama and Stark stay - they give Stark money and then he hands them something in return, either guns or what I quickly come to realize is drugs. The main house is always loud. People are always talking in booming voices, or yelling or laughing. There is no calmness or peace here. I have to always be alert; I can never rest and I'm so tired; not just my body, but my mind too. When the men are all together, they are always making noise. They shoot guns in the backyard at bottle targets or at nothing at all. They fight amongst themselves, punching and hurting each other over seemingly little. Seared into my memory is the night I saw Brew stab Gray in the arm over a card game. Gray was winning, and Brew accused him of cheating, whipping his knife out so fast that Gray didn't have a chance to react. Blood ran onto the table and all over his cards, while Brew and Stark laughed. Tru screamed and ran over to him, and Molly just sat there smirking. Mama sent me to get a towel, and when I brought it back, Brew grabbed my hand and held it over the puddle of blood on the table, teasing that he would put my hand in it. Brew and Stark were laughing, as I shrieked and tried to get away. Mama didn't laugh, but she didn't stop them. I didn't expect her to; I've always fought my battles on my own. I had nightmares about drowning in a river of blood for almost a month afterwards.

The men will also fight with the women, and hit them too. Mama is walking around with bruises. Sometimes I get bruises too. Stark is mean and rough. Mama says he doesn't mean to hurt us, but he never says sorry. He is always quick to lash out when he's angry. I can never do anything right. I try to stay away from him, but he always seems to catch me.

The radio is always on and turned up high; it plays almost constantly. If one of Daddy's songs ever comes on the radio, Mama will quickly switch the station. Stark seems to get mad when he hears Daddy sing. I think that he's jealous that my Daddy is a famous rock star and he is only a drug dealer and a criminal. I'm sad when Mama switches the station, but I get a small bit of satisfaction that it makes Stark upset.

There are no rules in this new life of Mama's; even less than there has ever been before. People eat and sleep whenever they want, and I follow suit. They might stay up all night and sleep all day, so that's what I do too. It is a life of chaos and uncertainty. I miss the structure of life with Uncle and Kate. There were rules to follow: bedtime at the same time every night, manners expected all the time, no yelling, be nice to each other...it feels better when you know what to expect from others. Everyone is so unpredictable here. I miss knowing what the rules are.

One night, the police do show up at the compound, and I'm hopeful for the first time in months. I see the flashing lights coming down the driveway and I feel so relieved. The loud scream of sirens causes pandemonium in house, but fills me with a sweet sense of relief. I can finally take a full breath for the first time in months. Uncle Freddie finally found me, and he's coming to get me and bring me back. Everyone in the house is panicking and rushing around trying to hide things, so they don't notice me waiting with a smile on my face. Just before the police break down the door, Mama shoves me into my little room, and tells me to keep my mouth closed or else. She closes the door and leans on it, so I can't get out. I don't plan on being quiet, I plan on screaming and yelling. However, it quickly becomes apparent that the police are not looking for me. They are looking for Brew. I don't know why and I don't care. I just want them to know that I'm here. I try yelling and banging on the door, but I can't be heard over the noise of arresting Brew – all the yelling, the police radios squawking, furniture being knocked over, and the din of the constantly loud radio. I bang on that door until my fists ache. My yells turn into gulping sobs and eventually I give up, defeated. I watch through the keyhole, as they roughly push Brew to the ground and then take him away in handcuffs and I whisper, "Take me too."

Months pass. My birthday isn't even acknowledged, so I make myself a little cake out of mud in yard and use a twig for a candle. I sing myself the birthday song and pretend to blow out my candle. Then I look up into the sky and tell Daddy it's my birthday. I wonder if he knows. I'm getting older and a bit taller now. I wonder if he would even recognize me. Mama says I'm becoming lady like, just like her. But I don't want to be like her, not ever; Mama is teaching me how not to be. I don't like the way these men are starting to look at me.

It is just before Christmas. I have been here with Mama for about 6 or 7 months. Time is crawling by, and I lose track of what day it is, what month it is. I'm so isolated here; it feels like I'm on another planet. I don't even remember what it was like to live at Uncle Freddie's anymore. I have made myself forget all those memories, as they only cause me pain. I have pushed them all out of my mind and just focus on getting through day after agonizing day.

One day, I come in after spending the afternoon with Tru, She has cut my hair and polished my nails. I like spending time with her, it is the only bright spot in this dismal place. Stark is gone and I find Mama crumpled on the kitchen floor in a heap. She is holding her head and crying quietly. I go over to her and kneel down.

"Mama?" I say quietly.

She notices me then, and tries to stand up quickly, but she can only stagger to her feet. I try to help her, but she pushes my hands away. She's embarrassed, and won't look at me. Her nose is bleeding and her lip is split. Her face has large red splotches, and so do her arms and collarbone, which will surely become big bruises. There are finger prints on her neck, and blood drops on her white t-shirt. She wipes her face with the back of her hand, smearing the blood from her nose and lips across her face. She touches her face tenderly and winces. She looks smaller and weaker than I've ever seen her.

"What happened?" I ask, but I already know. Stark's temper, and his behaviour, have become increasingly worse. I wonder how much longer before I would find myself in her place at his hands. She doesn't want to talk about it and tells me to scram. However, I can tell that something has changed in her. I know that it is only a matter of time now.

IX:

For better or for worse, we are on the run again. Mama wakes me up in the early morning hours about a month later, telling me to be very quiet and follow her. We are sneaking away with our suitcases while everyone is passed out or sleeping from the party the night before. We tip toe through the dark house, being careful not make any noise at all, freezing when Gray rolls over on the couch. If we are caught trying to leave, I can't imagine what will happen. My heart is pounding so hard, I'm afraid the whole house can hear it. He settles back down and begins snoring quietly. Mama looks towards the bedroom door to make sure it's not going to open. During the night, she had moved the car far up the long driveway, so starting it would not alert the others. She has planned this, waiting for the right time. We go out the back door, being careful to avoid the creaky stair at the bottom, and walk silently to the car. The night is still; the only sound in the dark are the crickets cheering us on, as she puts the suitcases in the back seat and closes the door with a quiet click. This is becoming the only routine Mama has – running away. But this time, I am more than happy to go with her.

She starts the car and we drive away, leaving that life in the rear view mirror, as we have left many others. I don't even look back. There is nothing to miss, not even Tru. I wonder how we will survive now, but Mama confides in me that she has stolen a lot of money from Stark in order to finance our getaway. When she says this, fear and panic race through my heart. It's drug money – it's a drug dealer's money obtained through crimes big and small, and I know that Stark will never let her get away with this. Not to mention the rest of the bikers; they will hunt her down, and she will forever have to look over her shoulder. She has now resigned herself to a life of hiding and fear, and by proxy, this will be my existence too. She continues to drag me deeper and deeper into her abyss of a life.

We spend a few nights in the car, as Mama is not sure what to do now and is trying to save the money she stole. She hasn't thought any farther ahead than escaping. I feel like we are sitting ducks, and every time I see a motorcycle or a sports car that looks like Krane's, I shake with fear. But as we get farther and farther away, the fear lessens just a bit. We have travelled into yet another state, going farther and farther East. Christmas is spent in a dingy little motel room along the highway. It is just another day.

We are now on the East Coast – a small North Carolina town where Mama grew up, a few hours drive away from the coast. She still has friends and family here, but there is no one she is really close with. In quick succession, we sleep on couches, in spare rooms, and on floors of various old friends, both male and female. It is a life of living out of a suitcase and always being ready to go at a moment's notice. We are never usually welcome for very long at each place, and Mama is never satisfied to stay long regardless. She is always wanting to move on to the next thing, the next place, the next adventure – always searching for something. I suspect she is searching for peace of mind, and the feeling of normalcy, but I don't think she will ever find it. She wouldn't recognize it even if she did. I know I'm not living a normal life, like other kids, but this is the only life I know. This is the only Mama I know.

In this place, I also begin to make friends. Mama feels safe and comfortable in her old hometown and since she has decided to stay in one place, she has enrolled me in school. It is my only escape. However, I am not used to a regimented lifestyle anymore and I'm not the best at attending regularly. I've become too independent and too unfazed by the little things like worrying about school and schoolwork, as I have spent too much time worrying about big things. Frankly, there is no one making sure I go, no one holding me accountable, so it all seems rather irrelevant. However, I do spend a lot of time in the music room, and it quickly becomes my favourite place in the world. It's the only place where I find some connection to Daddy, to my old life, and to what could have been before Mama put me on this crazy roller coaster.

I'm adept at several instruments, picking them up easily and learning them quickly; no doubt because Daddy encouraged me and tried to teach me when I was young. I tell a select few who my Daddy is and they are impressed. No one needs to know he's not my real Daddy. I also get to sing. I'm shy to do so in front of people at first, but I know I have a good voice. It's strong, and I'm told it's unique in pitch and timbre, with a husky raspiness that I can use or not use depending on the mood of the song. I don't hear unique, I just hear me, but when I sing, I find a new way of expressing myself through music and lyrics. I am at the same time vulnerable and wide open, but also controlled and guarded. I can show people as much or as little of myself as I want, expressed through my voice and the words I sing. I develop a mutual respect with the music teacher, Mr. Deacon, who is impressed with what he calls "my natural talent". He thinks I must get it from my Daddy, and I don't correct him. I also become quite close to another music room 'hang-arounder' named Eric. He's several years older than me; he's come back to finish high school, after dropping out years ago. It sounds like he has his own story to tell, and maybe I'll hear it some day. Eric plays guitar and sings, and has big dreams of being in a famous band one day. Something tells me he just might be able to pull it off; he's unbelievably talented. His fingers fly over the guitar strings, making it look effortless, and his voice is clear and pure, lending itself to any genre of song. He prefers hard rock though, and writes his own music.

As much as this place comes to mean to me and the close contacts I make here, I confide in no one about my situation. I am out of the mindset where I am waiting to be rescued and looking for help. I would be mortified now if anyone knew my story, so I keep quiet. I have found myself a little niche in life, and that's good enough for now. I am biding my time until...until when? Until I stop living Mama's life and can find my own.

Time is passing and I'm now 15. Mama continues to take off for a night or two here and there, enjoying the freedom that she lost when she lived under Stark's thumb. I'm not worried, I know she will come back, but it sure makes some of her friends mad when she leaves her kid with them and disappears. Through her friends, she is meeting a lot of new people. She finds herself a few boyfriends, one after the other, and convinces them to let us stay with them rather quickly. Some of them are nice enough, some are rather creepy. All are pretty much from the dredges of society. They are criminals and drug addicts and alcoholics. I'm not even sure which are actually boyfriends and which are just friends. They come and go from our lives, and we come and go from theirs. Mama treats them all the same, with the same fake familiarity, and tries hard to appease them so we have a place to stay. It is all about temporary survival. It has never occurred to Mama that she could survive on her own, if she just put as much effort and energy into that, as she does trying to find someone to take care of her.

Life goes on. There are bad times and there are even worse times. I can't really say there are any good times. I am going through the motions of a life, but not really living. We have spent three years bouncing around from place to place at a dizzying pace. I follow Daddy's career through the tv and magazines. I see how he is aging and changing in pictures. His hair is greying, he has grown a beard, but his eyes are the same. In those eyes, I see my past. I'm proud of him and his success and I wonder what his life is like without us, without me. Does he have a new family? Is he calling someone else his little girl? I was his first little girl. My heart still aches for him, but the ache has become smaller, dulled by the tears of disappointment. I'll always be a little girl left forgotten and unsaved by her hero, but I still smile and tear up when I hear 'Sunni, Honey'.

I have started looking forward to when I am free, picturing in precise detail how I will craft my life; it's almost within reach. I don't worry about what kind of house I will have or what kind of car I'll drive. People who have had their fundamental needs met all their lives have the luxury of pondering such things. No, I think about basic things that everyone else takes for granted. I think of what it will be like to have everything I don't have now like calmness, control, stability, and above all, love. My future will never include homelessness and transiency. I'll have a husband who will protect me when old nightmares resurface late at night. He will be strong enough to handle my demons, but soft enough to smother my children with hugs and kisses. And my children! They will feel like treasured gifts, not like burdens. They will know how important they are; their feelings and needs will never be disregarded. I'll surround them with a love I have never known, and they will not, for one moment, ever feel like I did. Everything in my life will be different. I will create the life I have yearned for. This dysfunction I'm living in will not go on – it stops with me, and I will do whatever it takes to ensure that.

Despite the dreams and goals I have, I'm afraid for my future, because I know that I have trouble connecting with other human beings. I crave human connection so desperately, but I honestly don't know if I will ever be able to achieve it. I've always lived in survival mode, so the walls I have built to protect myself seem impenetrable. Maybe I'm too independent, too street smart? And trust? Forget trust, nobody is to be trusted. Everyone will hurt you, everyone will disappoint you. This is my experience, but I don't want it to be my legacy. I'm very self aware, so I'm worried. I don't want to be alone, but I won't be needy and desperate like Mama. How will I strike a balance between my defense mechanisms and my happiness? It's that uncertainty that fuels my fear of letting anyone get close to me.

Mama has run out of people to stay with. She swallows her pride and calls her own Mama, whom she hasn't spoken to in a long time. I feel she must have a good reason for not being close with her Mama, but I do not ask. She has no desire to share her secrets with me, and I've always learned everything I need to know through observation. Words don't mean anything anyway. I give her privacy, because I know this is really hard for her to do.

She has a long conversation, full of anger and tears, before she hangs up and tells me I am going to meet my Grandmother. I don't have a good feeling about this, but Mama is determined to try, out of sheer desperation.

My Grandmother lives just outside of town, not too far away. She knows about me, but has never seen me. Mama has not spoken to her in a long time. Something happened to cause a rift, but I don't know what; that is her business and I don't need to share in any more of her burdens. We arrive at her Mama's house, on a pretty, tree-lined street in a quiet neighbourhood, late in the evening. As we pull in the small paved driveway, I see her looking out the window, waiting for us. The one story house is sided in wooden clapboard, with green shutters and a green front door. Manicured hedges surround the front of the house and line the walkway, and flower beds in front of the house are blooming in colour. She opens the door and ushers us inside. Mama puts down her bags in the entrance way and they just stand there staring awkwardly at each other for a moment. They don't hug, but Mama manages to say, "It's been a long time. You're looking well."

Grandmother nods, an air of aloofness about her. She is a

small woman, slightly shorter than Mama and I. Her long grey hair was once blonde, and is pulled away from her face and tucked behind her ears. She is in a pale blue dressing gown and matching slippers, holding a cane in one hand. She was beautiful once, but time has worn on her face, making her look tired and cross. She must have spent a lot of time with her brows furrowed, because the lines there are deeply etched. I sense that life wasn't easy for her either. It seems to run in the family, every generation passing on their struggle to the next.

She looks at me. I am unable to read the look on her face. Mama introduces me. Grandmother sniffs and nods again, saying to me "You can call me Louise." There is to be no acceptance here.

The first night we are there, Louise sets me up on a pull out couch in the spare room. It is another bed in another strange place. I'm used to it. It's not the best accommodations, but certainly not the worst. Grandmother's... Louise's... house is small, but tidy and in good repair. She lives here alone, and is still well enough to take care of herself.

As I lay there drifting asleep, I hear them talking in the living room At first, I can just hear the din of conversation, unable to make out any words. Louise and Mama argue back in forth in hushed tones, until one or the other's voices raise and that's when I can hear a bit of what it being said. I quickly piece together what they are talking about. I learn part, but I'm sure not all, of their story. Years ago, Mama had accused Louise's third husband of touching her, hurting her. Louise insists that Mama is lying, and did so out of spite to break up the marriage. She says Mama was jealous. Mama insists that what she accused him of is true, and she is so angry that Louise didn't believe her. She says Louise never believed her and she was forced to leave home. She talks of being physically abused by both Louise and her husbands, that all of them were a bunch of drunks, but Louise vehemently denies this.

Mama tells Louise that she was never a good mother. I wonder if she knows how ironic this statement is. I hear Louise growl that Mama was always a troublemaker and no one believed her wild stories. Their voices raise and lower late into the night. I fall asleep imagining what Mama's life must have been like when she was young, but I just can't muster up any sympathy for her. I feel bad for that.

Mama and Louise argue constantly during the time we are there. Everyone is miserable, and I'm surprised the accommodations last as long as they do. I think Mama honestly hoped to reconcile with her mother, but there was too much water under the bridge...and the bridge was on fire.

Towards the end, Mama started not returning to the house at nights. I didn't know where she was, but I had a feeling she either met someone, or was trying to meet someone in order to have somewhere else to go. When I was alone with Louise, it was uncomfortable. She didn't speak to me much, didn't seem interested in me or my life, nor did she wish to know how Mama had been living these past years. This was supposed to be family, my blood relative, but it was no more comfortable here than it was staying at any of the other numerous places we've been. In some ways, family can be colder than strangers.

We lasted at Louise's for about three weeks. Mama was crawling out of her skin with the need to get away from her. The tension in the house was unbearable. Louise wasn't sorry to see us go. Mama admitted to me later that this would likely be the last time she ever saw her mother. I wondered if I would ever see my Daddy again.

X:

We are now staying in a shelter, but Mama has been gone more often than not. Sometimes she doesn't come back in the evening and they give her bed away to someone else. I go to school in the day and back to shelter at night. It is a dreary existence. I'm barely passing my classes, because my mind is too full to care about the meaningless things happening at school. I don't make many friends; I mostly keep to myself. I just can't relate to the giggling teenage girls with their seemingly perfect lives, talking about boys, parties and vacations. They fret over hairstyles and clothes, and other things that I just don't have the ability to care about. I just can't relate, so I don't even try.

My saving grace, and the only thing that keeps me going back, is that music room and Eric. I learn that he is 22, and has returned to school determined to finish so he can graduate, in case his dreams of stardom with his band don't come true. However, his main focus is his music. We often stay late, alone in the music room and just talk, about everything and nothing at all. I find Eric easy to talk to, but I keep my secrets to myself. I fear if I open up too much, he will decide I have too much baggage and won't want to waste his time with me anymore. Maybe it's an irrational fear, but it's real to me. It's ingrained in me. I need to keep my life to myself, no one can know the real me. The real me is not good enough, not worthy enough. I deal with my own stuff.

I often think that Eric would like to be more than just a friend; I think he likes me differently than I like him. But, I don't have the mental energy to entertain a relationship. I don't have any room in my life or any space in my head to invite anyone in. I have the weight of the world on my shoulders and I must carry it alone. I just need a friend. I've always needed a friend...but sometimes I like the way he flicks his long dark hair out of face when he's playing guitar.

Eric has lived on his own ever since his stepfather kicked him out of the house when he was 17. They didn't get along, and his mother chose to side with her husband. Life at home was full of arguments and tension, and he finally left after a particularly heated argument resulted in a fight where his stepfather punched him in the face. He is now estranged from most of the family, save for an uncle. He doesn't talk about his family much – we don't ask each other a lot of questions. We just exist together and enjoy having someone who makes us feel not alone in the world. I do share one thing with him. He knows that I haven't seen Daddy in a long time and I miss him so much. I don't go into the whole story, but he knows Mama took me when I was little and left in the night. I know that I can trust him, but I don't share much more. I go over to his house a lot, it gets me away from the shelter, and Mama is not too interested in keeping track of me anyway. The small one bedroom house is owned by his uncle, who charges him very little rent in exchange for repairs and upkeep. Eric has a part-time job at a local gas station to supplement the money he makes playing gigs at weddings or other events. He's scratching out an existence, barely getting by, but he's making it on his own and living his own life. I'm jealous of his independence and freedom. He's not tied to anyone, no one is dragging him down. One day, somehow, I'll achieve that too.

We often sit in his garage and I listen to him sing and play guitar. I like the intense look of concentration he gets on his face when he gets lost in his music; the far away look in his eyes like he can see his future in the melodies. He's going to make it, I can feel it. We write lyrics together and he puts music to it. His band comes over to practice and they put our words into song. It is the most beautiful process. I know what Daddy felt now, and I understand his need to surround himself with his art. It's been so many years; so much has happened. I want to reach out to him, but I wouldn't even know what to say. I spend my 16th birthday with Eric, and for the first time in many years, I have a real birthday cake and someone to share it with.

On a rainy Saturday night, Eric shows me a newspaper clipping. Daddy's band will be playing in the neighbouring city next week, only a half hour away. My heart fills with excitement and fear. Never has he been so close and within such easy reach. Do I dare? Eric says what will it hurt to go see him play? But it will hurt. It will hurt for the past - for all the lost time, for all the memories that were never made, and a for life that veered horribly off course and never recovered...and it might hurt in the present – for heartbreak that I couldn't survive if I was rejected. I have handled a lot of stuff in my young years, but I am totally incapable of coping if Daddy dismisses me. He has been the only thing I have hung onto all these years to keep me sane. Maybe it's better to leave well enough alone – to keep hope alive even if it's never attained, instead of finding out there is no hope at all. I'm terrified of trying and I'm terrified of not trying. I'm frozen.

Eric spends the better part of the week trying to convince me to go to the concert – just to be in the audience – to see Daddy in person. He says at least I will be there to have the choice to reach out to him or not. If I'm not there, I have no choice. This is my one chance.

In the end, I let Eric get tickets. I don't tell Mama when I see her in passing as she comes and goes at the shelter. Another secret to keep, but this one tingles inside me, instead of the usual cumbersome secrets I hold. Mama has no clue how I spend my time, she never asks. She just takes for granted that I'll always be around, and I am. Maybe one day I won't be.

I do know that Mama is still very afraid of Stark finding her; she keeps her eyes open and stays on alert. She doesn't want to be found. She has committed an unforgivable and dangerous act by stealing that money. Just as important, she carries the knowledge of all his crimes. The information she has about him, his friends and their sins frightens her. She has had a lot of time to think, and she is well aware of the full weight of her actions. It is obvious that she's changed since leaving Stark; she's not the same person anymore. Instead of being carefree and spontaneous, she's anxious all the time and startles easily. She's also developed nervous habits, and has been medicating herself again from another unlabelled pill bottle she got from someone. Her stress and worries show on her face. Mama has aged very quickly in the past several months. That's what your conscience can do to you I suppose. When she's around, she's serious and always deep in thought. I don't know what she does when she's not around. I assume she's living hand to mouth and taking whatever she can get from those around her. It's the only way she's ever known how to live.

The week ends with Eric and I hopping on a bus to go to the concert. The bus ride is quiet – we don't talk. I am simultaneously grateful to Eric, and also mad at him for giving me this opportunity. Part of me wishes he just hadn't told me about the concert at all, hadn't put the idea in my head, and then I would be none the wiser. Everything would be the same, and not potentially on the verge of change. Change is scary, and I've been through too much of it in my life.

We get to the venue, a large arena on the outskirts of town, after walking from the bus station. Our seats are centre stage, but many rows back. I will not be spotted in the audience. I am anonymous. I wait nervously, impatiently, through the opening act. I'm shaking with fear, why am I so scared? Eric tries to show his support by holding my hand, but I pull away and pull my hands up into the sleeves of my jean jacket. I need to be alone in this moment, but I also need him here. He seems to understand without me having to say it.

Finally the lights dim even more and the stage lights up with flashing colours. The crowd starts to roar loudly. Everyone around me is yelling and cheering, a sea of smiling, carefree faces around me. They have no idea of my turmoil and how big this moment is for me.

I jump, startled, as a booming voice comes across the loudspeaker, "And now ladies gentlemen, give a warm welcome to Graham Sage and the Night Winds!"

And then I see him - for the first time in seven years, or is it eight? Daddy walks onto the stage, carrying his guitar, followed by his band. He waves to the crowd, as he takes his place at the microphone. He looks the same, he looks different. He looks older. He looks like love, and he looks like a million memories of time gone by. I am mesmerized and I feel Eric watching me. I subconsciously lean into him a little bit for support. He puts an arm around my shoulders and I let it stay there.

Daddy greets the crowd and I hear his voice for the first time. It sounds so different than hearing him on the radio. Instantly I'm reminded of all the bedtime stories and songs and conversations of my childhood, of the "I love you's" and "Sleep tight Princess"es. There is a lump in my throat. He is still talking to the crowd, but I don't hear the words. I am lost in my own words from the past.

The crowd quiets down a bit as he begins to sing. He is singing songs I don't recognize. Newer music that I've never heard. It hurts that I'm so out of the loop and don't know these songs, but it is distinctively Daddy's writing and Daddy's sound. The crowd is singing along. It is all so surreal. He is singing about lonesome highways and long, lonely nights; of full moons and sad smiles. After the ballad is over, he launches right into some harder rock with a classic sound, stamping his foot to the music. He has a big smile on his face as he sings. It's easy to see how much he loves it all.

I pull my eyes away from him just for a moment and smile when I see that Sticks is still on the drums. It is a familiar face from time gone by. I also recognize the keyboard player, but not the bass player. The back up singers are pretty, but older looking women. I wonder if one of them is Daddy's new wife.

Eric is nudging me forward in the crowd, closer to the stage. I look at him and shake my head no, no, no... but he says, "Just a little bit" and I let him lead me through the maze of people until we are a bit closer to the stage. The music plays on; my eyes are glued to Daddy, and I'm lost in the past. When the music stops, Daddy begins telling a story, tales of life on the road and how and why some of his songs were written. I wonder if he will make eye contact with me if I keep staring at him. And if he did, would he know who I was? I'm very different than the little girl he last saw hanging over her mother's shoulder on the way out the door, through the tears in his eyes.

The crowd cheers, music plays...and before I'm ready for it to be, the show is almost over. Daddy is winding up, thanking the crowd, telling them how much he enjoyed playing for them. As he speaks, I hear the familiar beginning notes...

Daddy starts to sing, "Sunni, honey, the sky's not blue without you...Sunni, honey, the ocean's don't roar when you're not near... Sunni, honey, the birds don't sing and the sun doesn't shine...Sunni, honey, I'm sure glad you're mine..."

Tears are streaming down my face. Eric looks at me but says nothing. He knows how hard this is for me.

Daddy continues the song that made him a household name, easily his most recognizable song. My name is sung by the hundreds of people around me in unison. The whole experience is so bizarre, so unreal...it's like I'm floating on the ceiling watching myself and watching it all happen.

The song ends and the band stops playing. Daddy shouts an "I love you" to the crowd and he and the band start walking off the stage. Eric is grabbing my hand and pulling me through the crowd. They are all headed towards the exit, but we are headed the opposite way, further into the arena, towards the backstage door. I stop instantly when I realize what he's doing.

"Eric...I... I can't..." I'm so overwhelmed right now. This isn't the right time or the right place for this, but on the other hand, it's the only time and place for this. My heart is beating so fast, I feel like I'm going to faint.

"You can do this!" Eric urges. He pulls me forward.

We don't make it much farther. The backstage is crawling with security guards and they are busy throwing out some girls who have tried to sneak in. They see us and come towards us, motioning for us to leave.

Eric pipes up and says, "Can you tell Graham that his daughter is here to see him!"

I stare at him. I can't stop what's happening right now.
The security guards scoff, not believing him, pointing us to the door.

Eric yells, "Graham!" really loud, but there's so much noise, it won't be heard by Daddy.

As they are physically pushing us towards the door, Eric pleads one last time, "Please tell Graham that Sunni Ducayne was here to see him. Make sure you do that!"

They nod and close the door behind us and we are outside in the cold of the night. We have been pushed out the side door of the building and we are alone in the quiet.

"Damn," Eric kicks the ground. I stuff my hands in my pockets to warm them up. I can't stop shaking, but it's not from the cold.

Eric thinks for a moment, then grabs my hand again and starts to run. He is running us around to the back of the building. There, the tour bus is parked, along with other vehicles. A few crew members are mulling around outside smoking. He stops and crouches down behind a black pick up truck, out of ear shot of the people.

"What are you doing? What is your plan? Were you planning to sneak us on the bus?" I am exasperated, what is he thinking?!

"Of course not. We're just going to hang out here until he comes out."

My panic is rising again. We're going to get caught. We should just leave, but we have to stay. This is it. When he comes out for a smoke, or to go back on the bus, we can call out to him before anyone can send us away. I terrified. What if he ends up being the one that sends us away? My heart would shatter into a million pieces.

We wait out there for a long time, crouched down behind the vehicle, keeping an eye on the door. People are coming in and out for smoke breaks or fresh air, none of which were Daddy. They are talking and laughing - most are roadies, I imagine, as they are carrying out and loading equipment into a big cube van. We wait so long. It's getting late, and it's getting too cold to stay out here.

"We need to give up," I sigh.

But Eric won't be discouraged. He stands up out of our hiding spot and starts walking towards the crew. What is he doing? My heart is pounding, but I follow along slowly, several paces behind him.

He approaches the first guy he sees, who is standing off by himself crushing his cigarette into the ground.

"Hey!" Eric calls. The man turns and looks at him. I expect to see security guards running at us. He acknowledges Eric with a nod. "I'm looking for Graham." Eric says.

The guy shakes his head and says, "Not sure if you're trying to stalk him or what, but Graham isn't here anymore."

"But the bus is here."

"Graham doesn't stay after the show. He leaves as soon as the show is over. He's halfway to the next venue by now. We travel with two buses. He's long gone." The man turns and walks away.

My heart sinks in my chest with disappointment, but also a small bit of relief. A dark sadness settles over me. Then I get angry. So many emotions flood over me all at once.

"Let's get out of here." I turn and walk away. Eric follows with his head hanging down.

1988-1991: The Traumatic Years

I:

Well, Mama has surprised me – just when I didn't think it was possible. Her unpredictable behaviour is normally always predictable. She is always easy for me to read, and although she constantly disappoints me, she never surprises me. Until now.

Mama eloped the day before with a man she met only a couple months prior. She dropped this bomb on me early one morning, when she pulled up in the car as I was walking to school. She opened the door and motioned for me to get in. This is still the same car that we left Daddy in, that we've slept in countless nights, that's taken us thousands of miles from home. When I look in that car, I just see pain...I don't want to get in...but Mama is blocking traffic and people are starting to honk at her. I reluctantly get in the front seat and she drives us to a restaurant down the road, offering to get us breakfast. I'm usually always hungry, there has never been enough food in my life, and definitely never a lot of full hot meals, so I agree.

As we sit at the table waiting for food, Mama explains how it has taken her a long time, but she finally managed to get legally divorced from Daddy, in absentia, some time ago. I had no idea. This finality upsets me for reasons I can't understand. It cements the fact that Daddy is not only gone, but legally gone. He's not my biological father and he's not even my legal father anymore. Any connection at all has been severed permanently. My heart hurts – our new legal status is a giant chasm.

Mama says I'm getting older now and I need to understand things from her point of view, but I don't have to understand anything. Her point of view is selfish and self-serving; it always has been. I don't have to understand any of the choices she has made. All her choices and behaviour have done is made me miserable and unhappy – a lifelong journey of mental anguish and physical deprivation. She has insisted on dragging me through her train wreck of a life, instead of doing the kind thing and leaving me where I would have been loved and cared for with Uncle Freddie...or with Daddy...or at a foster home, for heaven's sake. Instead, she selfishly kept me with her and irreparably changed who I am and what I could have been. I cannot understand. I refuse to understand. She's right about one thing, I am older now, older and wise beyond my years, and I don't forgive and forget.

I stay silent as she tells me about her new husband Buddy. Buddy is wrestler on the local circuit. A wrestler...I shake my head in disbelief and dismay...what has this woman been up to when she's been disappearing? She explains that she met him at the arena after a show. She was there with some girlfriends and they hung around like teenage groupies, by the sounds of it. She says Buddy is a wonderful man – I highly doubt this, as she has proven time and again that her standards are not very high.

She goes on to say he has a nice house with plenty of room and he is expecting us both to live with him. I am welcome to join them and be a real family. He doesn't have any other children, so it will just be the three of us. She says he makes a fine living and while we won't be rich, we won't want for anything anymore. He is offering her a life of stability and she is taking him up on it, even if I don't. She says it is my choice – I'm welcome to make my own way in life if I wish, or I can come and live with them. She is basically willing to abandon me to a life on the streets to fend for myself. I seriously consider fending for myself, as it may be the better option. There would be benefits to severing ties with her and her new life. In the end, I'm still only 16 and I have nowhere to go. I have no way to support myself and only one real friend in the world, and I'm not going impose upon him and drag his life down while he is trying to make something of himself. I find out that Buddy actually lives fairly close to Eric and this does please me. I think long and hard, and I really I have no other choice when it comes right down to it. Against my better judgment, and with nothing but trepidation in my heart, I reluctantly agree to stay on the roller coaster I have been riding with Mama.

Buddy lives in a modest, older two story house with brown vinyl siding and a wooden front porch painted white. There is a double car garage attached to the house, with one side left open. There's no lawn, no grass, just a wide open area of dirt leading up to the house. It is the last house at the end of a dead end street in an older neighbourhood, backing onto a wooded area. Being several blocks away from Eric's place, he is within walking distance now.

Buddy isn't home when we get there. Mama proudly gives me a tour of the house, as though she has bought and paid for it with her own money. Walking in the front door, the first thing I see is the back door, located in the kitchen at the back of the house. There is a long hallway in between, to the right of which is the living room and to the left are the steps upstairs. The bedrooms are upstairs, separated by the bathroom. Mama shows me the spare bedroom which will now be mine. I look out the window and see her car below. I must admit, although it's an older house, this is much nicer accommodations that we've had in a long time. I haven't had a room to myself since we left Daddy and I am looking forward to the privacy.

Buddy comes home in time for supper and I meet him for the first time. He is a rather homely man with curly blonde hair. He's stocky and not at all like the athletic wrestler I was picturing. I'm a little surprised, but maybe this is a good sign. He's quiet, but he seems nice enough. I don't get a vibe from him that he's annoyed to have me there, like I've felt so many times before. I have a sixth sense for those subtle signs that I am a third wheel, and I honestly don't feel any with him. I'm hopefully optimistic as the evening goes on. We eat pizza and have a few laughs getting to know each other. Maybe, just maybe Mama finally made a good choice, and if she did, it was surely accidental. He seems to treat her well enough, but I am cognizant of the fact that everything is still pretty new. I settle in to my new room, sleeping alone in a room by myself for the first time in quite a long time. The silence is unnerving at first, as I'm used to the constant noise of the shelter. The only noise I can hear is the sound of crickets. I fall asleep praying to the universe that Mama has finally done something right... and that she won't do something to mess it up. I don't think I have another midnight flight in me.

Over the following weeks, I watch Mama trying to be the perfect housewife, cooking and cleaning like she never did before. If she only made this much effort with Daddy my life might have been different. So, it actually makes me a bit angry to see her playing Suzie Homemaker all of a sudden. When I'm with Eric, I admit to him that this bothers me. He says he understands why I would feel this way. He is supportive without trying to tell me how to fix my problems. He just listens.

All is not perfect in this world though. Buddy drinks... a lot and every night. He's frequently drunk, but he is not an angry or scary drunk. Maybe this is just a compromise I'm going to have to put up with in order to have this semi-normal life. As long as he's not mean when he's drunk, maybe it will be okay. Mama drinks with him, more than I've ever seen her drink before. I stay to myself and out their way. This is just a place to stay – this is not the cozy nuclear family I've always yearned for. The time for that has long since passed. It's alright though, it makes it easier to steel myself against developing any sort of connection with Buddy. It justifies my unwillingness to care about him. He is not a substitute for Daddy any more than any of the other strangers who came in and out of my life. Just because they are legally married, and even if he really is a good man, it still won't change my allegiance to the only father I know.

Buddy has no family close by, and he's pretty much a loner. He does have one close friend, whom I meet within the first week; Michael also wrestles in the local circuit. I don't like

Michael from the first moment I set eyes on him. He's a good 10 years or more younger than Buddy, and much taller, at least 6'3. His height, along with his long dirty blonde hair and beard, make him look intimidating, but it's his attitude and the creepy vibe he strongly exudes that makes the hair on the back of my neck stand up. I try to be friendly at first, but the way he leers at me whenever I'm around is unnerving. I make myself scarce when he's over. I get the feeling he's used to hanging around the house a lot. He comes over at all hours of the day or night; we can hear his big noisy truck coming from way down the road. He just walks in without knocking and sits down, totally comfortable, and stays for hours. I don't know what Mama thinks of him. I think she's willing to accept whatever she has to so that she doesn't lose the quality of life she's found. So most nights, the three of them sit and drink together into the wee hours of the morning. I stay upstairs in my room with my door locked and a chair under the doorknob, just in case.

I've discovered that I can get out of the house by climbing out my window onto the porch roof below and jumping down to the ground. This way, I don't draw attention to myself when I'm coming or going, because Michael feels the need to hug or touch me in some way every time he sees me. He teases me and makes dirty jokes, and I don't like it. I need to stay far away from him.

I come and go as I like out the bedroom window, still counting on Mama's lack of maternal instinct and supervision. I do as I please and she doesn't seem to care. I pretty much do as I please as she does not seem to care. She doesn't realize that I'm still basically a child and shouldn't be left to my own devices like an adult. She has never fulfilled her role since I was born, so why would she start now. I used to think that she was lucky that I wasn't an out of control, rebellious kid, getting into all sorts of trouble because of her lax parenting. I could have caused her all sorts of problems if I went down a different path, or took my anger out on the world, instead of keeping it bottled inside. But now I realize that I'm the lucky one. Any bad behaviour would not affect her, it would only serve to ruin my life, and I haven't even had a chance to live yet.

Eric's band, "The Derelicts", and their music are starting to become recognized locally. They are doing a lot of gigs at various events, and bars, as well as opening for bigger name acts at the local concert hall. He's so happy, and I'm so proud of him. He might actually be able to make a living off his music one day. He remains the only person in the world who understands me, who I feel the need to have in my life. He still wants to be more than just a friend. He thinks he is waiting for me to come to my senses and realize that's what I want too, but my feelings are a mystery even to me. I'm so far removed from myself that I can't seem to find my way back. I feel nothing, but I feel everything.

II:

I am 17 now. Mama has been married to Buddy for almost a year. Life is moving along and I feel like I'm just an observer watching it pass by. I'm just a ghost in my own life. I hide in the shadows in my own house to avoid Michael. He just outright stares me up and down now, and he gets mean when I reject his advances or push him away. He makes my skin crawl and I think that he could be dangerous.

Something isn't right with Mama. There has been a few occasions that she has went out and not come home for a day or two – once it was almost a week. Her old habits and patterns seem to be returning. Maybe she isn't happy here after all. I'm not sure what is going on with her, but I pack a suitcase and keep it under the bed just in case. I would like to have a better relationship with her, but she makes it impossible to get close. I'll never know what's going on in her head, so I can only watch and wait. When I was little, I always thought that things would get better once I was older, and we were on more of a level playing field. Maybe she'd relate to me better when I could understand more, when she could be more of a friend than a mother. Sadly, that hasn't happened, and I have given up hope that it will. She remains as distant as ever.

I have been keeping track of Daddy's life through magazines and newspaper interviews to find out what's happening with him. I can't just let him go. It would be so much easier if I could. It's hard to forget about him when his face and his music are everywhere. His career has skyrocketed and he has become an internationally known rock star. He tours constantly, travelling the world. I am in awe of what he has achieved since those days of jamming with his band in the music room in the basement. Maybe he was better off without us. Maybe his life was meant to take the turn it did so that he could reach the heights he has. Maybe the universe aligned things for him by getting rid of us.

Daddy said in a recent interview that he still lives in the house his career began in, so that means he's still in our old house; he hasn't moved. He was always a simple man, with simple needs, and I'm not surprised that he hasn't let his money and his fame go to his head. He wasn't the type that needed to spend his money lavishly. I can't see him buying houses and cars and living like a rich person. He's always taken his fame in stride. It's always been all about the love of music for him. He just wants people to hear his songs. For him, family would always be first. The fame is secondary. I would have been first, if I was still in his life.

A tv entertainment news program that I watch late one night informs me that Daddy has indeed remarried, but only fairly recently – four years ago. He has two stepsons, but no children of his own. I don't know why, but that makes me feel better. I don't want to share him, even though I'm not able to share him anyway. That is nonsensical, but that is how my mind works. I watch the reporter speak about him, with his picture on the screen in the background. His wife's name is Maria and my suspicions were correct, she does sing background vocals for him. She was on stage with him the night Eric and I saw him in concert. A picture of them together replaces the picture of him in the report. She is pretty enough, long blonde hair, tall and slim. I compare her to Mama, but I don't know what that does for me. Her sons Travis and Brian are both older than me and one still lives at home with them. I still think of Daddy as his younger self – who he was when we left him about 9 or 10 years ago now. Daddy is older than Mama by a few years, so he would be 49 years old now. I have missed a whole decade of his life, and he has missed a whole decade of mine. Time has gone by so fast, and it can't ever be recovered...and it hurts.

I want to reach out to him, but now knowing that someone

else could answer the phone discourages me even more. Maria might not even know about me. If I were to try to contact him, how would he explain me? I'm not even his real child. I have no claim on him. It might even cause problems in his marriage. He doesn't deserve to have me ruining his life twice. So, I continue to be just an observer, watching other people live what would have been my life.

Mama is gone again. I've avoided the house for over a week now, waiting for her to come back. I stay with Eric sometimes. He wishes I would stay permanently, but I don't want to impose on his life too much. He has a lot going on right now trying to get his career of the ground. I give him his space, because I think he might get tired of having me around, like people seem to have done all my life. I feel inconsequential to everyone, and if Eric ever did tire of me and I didn't have him in my life, I don't know how I would be coping right now. And honestly, I'm afraid to get too close. Trying to connect with another human being doesn't come easily for me. As someone who has never had any connections before, it's terrifying. So I find other places, and other people to stay with too, convinced I am doing the right thing by keeping a bit of distance between Eric and I. I'm not proud when it dawns on me that I am just like Mama – bouncing from place to place, and doing some things I'm not proud of and aren't ready to do, in order to avoid having to go home at night. I come back to the house every day, to watch for her car or any sign of her. I need to be here when she comes back or she may leave without me. I am tied to her with an invisible string, and I don't know why, and I don't know how to sever it.

I have to avoid the house every night because I know Buddy and Michael will be there and will be drunk, with or without Mama. I only needed to see Michael drunk once to know that I can never, ever be around him again. As horrible as he is sober, he is even worse drunk. He's mean and violent. At a house party one night, Michael got into a fight with someone in the backyard, beating the guy to a bloody pulp. He relentlessly pounded him over and over with a crazed look on his face. He was out of control and it took two men to pull him off. He was also hitting on the all the women, including Mama, touching and kissing them and ignoring their protests. Life with Mama has exposed me to the most horrible people, and she's unapologetic for it all.

I was lucky to escape my childhood relatively unscathed by the men Mama has brought around. Although, to be fair, my line in the sand as to what is acceptable and unacceptable treatment is pretty murky and some of my memories are hazy; others I have pushed out of my mind completely. In all honesty I don't even know how unscathed I really am; I have just played the hand I've been given. My childhood is a blur of people and places – and if I think really hard, some of those people may not have been so nice after all. So I don't let myself think too much.

Going on three weeks and Mama has not returned. I need to speak to Buddy to about it. He is drinking already at ten in the morning when I go to the house to see him. He does admit that he's worried about her. So am I, she has never been gone this long, except when she left me with Uncle Freddie. We don't know what to do. He refuses to call the police and tells me not to bother either. He's not interested in being their radar, but I don't ask why. Plus, Mama has taken off on him before, and I confirm that she has taken off many times on me over the years and she has always comes back. He worries that maybe she left him for someone else and, although I don't say anything to him, I feel that this might indeed be what has happened. If so, she should at least be coming back for me. She always comes back for me. I will just keep waiting.

When I'm at Eric's, we lay side by side in the bed, not touching, staring at the ceiling in the dark and just talking until we fall asleep. I feel obligated to sleep with him, as payment for the accommodations, so he will let me keep hanging around. When I tell him this, he doesn't understand and he gets upset with me. He says he doesn't expect anything and will never pressure me. He doesn't let me repay him this way, and I'm not expecting that reaction. What he doesn't understand is that I have been taught that everyone has a currency. Everything, every place, has a price, and if I don't pay it, I might lose him. When Mama didn't pay the price where she was staying – whether it was following the rules at Uncle Freddie's, being a good friend to Marva, being expected to forgive her own mother for her mistreatment, or how I'm sure many men in her life expected her to pay – she would have to leave and lose those people from her life. I can't lose Eric, even thought I'm not sure of my feelings for him – how much I care for him versus how much I need him. That's not fair to him, but that's self preservation. I'm forever in survival mode, so I can't even figure out how I actually feel about him. How messed up am I...

We had the biggest celebration when he and the band get signed to a label and are going to make their first real album. We also celebrated the fact that we have both managed to graduate high school, me by the skin of my teeth, despite the chaos of my life and my lack of attendance. I told Mama, wanting to share something good with her. She said congratulations, and then showed me her new shade of nail polish. Despite her response, I'm pretty proud of that diploma, but I don't attend the ceremony. There's no point, and there's no one to be proud of me anyway, except Eric. So we celebrate our success together with Chinese takeout and that's good enough.

So now, I need to find some way to make money. I'm tired of feeling like I'm sponging off Eric and I don't want to be accused of sponging off Buddy in Mama's absence. I manage to get a job working with a road crew, setting up and taking down the lights and equipment for local concerts. I also learn a lot about electronics and troubleshooting equipment problems. It's not much, but it's something that keeps me in the music business. I am able to make some money doing some background vocals and demos as well. Maybe one day I'll be able to get songwriting credit. I'm happy having my foot in the door of the music world. Maybe my plan to run into Daddy somewhere along the way will come true one day.

I bury myself in my work and in the music, and the weeks fly by. I'm happy to have something to focus on. Eric wants me to sing a duet with him which would be on his new album, but I don't wish to do any lead vocals. I want to stay behind the scenes. I'm not looking for fame, I just want to experience what Daddy feels when he's around music. Daddy, on the other hand, has achieved the ultimate in fame. His face and music are everywhere: on t-shirts, hats, posters in every store. He constantly has a song on the music charts in the top ten. He spends months on the road touring around the country and overseas. I haven't managed to cross paths with him yet, but I have met some mutual acquaintances. I tell them I am his daughter only because I'm hoping the word gets back to him. I'm testing the waters, hoping he reaches out to me. I'm afraid to pursue him in case he doesn't want anything to do with me, but I do get his personal number from his former manager who I run into at business party - after making up a story that I couldn't hear him on the phone when he was trying to give me his number due to the poor connection he had while he was in Japan. Ever since, I've been so tempted to call that I'm crawling out of my skin. A million times I have picked up the phone and started to dial. A million times I have hung up before it connects.

III:

Mama where are you? It's now been months. Summer is almost over and no sign of her. I see Buddy regularly. He doesn't seem to mind me coming and going from the house. He's pretty aloof, and seems content to wait and see if Mama comes back or not. He works, he drinks...he hangs around with Michael. He's a simple man. On one hand I'm worried about Mama, but on the other hand, I wonder if she is just being the ultimate in selfish by disappearing completely and not coming back for me. This is a legitimate possibility, so I let anger triumph over worry. I'm sure she's fine. She's living a new life and apparently no longer has room for me in it. I don't need her anyway, what has she ever done for me? When she comes back we are going to have it out once in for all. I let my anger fester, but a little voice in the back of my head is quietly troubled.

On a cool late Autumn afternoon I'm doing laundry at Buddy's, and the noise of the machine masks the sound of the big black truck coming down the road. I hear the door of the house open and close, and I freeze. I hope it's Buddy; would be nice if it's Mama. Soon I can tell by the heavy clunk of cowboy boots that it is Michael. I've always been afraid that he might come over when I'm here alone. I need to get out the back door before I'm seen, but as I tip toe into the kitchen I find Michael sitting at the kitchen table, beer in hand. He smirks at me.

"Well, well... I thought I heard someone when I came in. Thought it might be your Mama. She ever come back yet? Do you miss yer Mama, Sunni?" His look is not one of concern, the smirk sits plastered on his face.

I reach for the door knob and open the door. He's on his feet pulling the door out of my hand and slamming it closed again.

What happens next is not something I want to remember in

detail. Suffice to say I run towards the other door, but he easily catches me in the hallway and slams me up against the wall. He holds me there with a big forearm across my collarbones, pressing against my neck. He's so much bigger than me, and over a foot taller. I'm struggling to get out of his grip and he's kissing my neck and face, and his hands are all over me, down my pants and under my shirt. I push him away and start to scream, but he covers my mouth with his hand. I manage to bite one of his fingers as hard as I can, and it's enough to make him loosen his grip just a bit. I try to run again but now he's angry. He punches me right in the face and my nose instantly starts to bleed all over both of us. A couple more punches and my lip is split and my eye is swelling. He's on top of me on the floor; he has gotten my pants down and is undoing his own. He's holding my legs open by kneeling between them. He's so much bigger and stronger than me. I feel like I can't breathe. I kick and scream and scratch and bite. I fight with all my might for this not to happen. He's trying...he's trying...but he can't...he can't do it...he physically can't do it...and that is the only thing that saves me. He's angry. He leaves me lying on the floor and storms out of the house. I breath a sigh of relief when I hear his truck start up and drive off.

I sit up, dazed, wiping blood out of my eyes. I'm in shock and I'm shaking. It takes me a moment to come to my senses. I don't know if he's coming back so I have to get myself together and out of the house fast. I stagger to my feet, wincing in pain. My face is throbbing, and the coppery taste of blood is on my tongue. Making my way upstairs as quickly as I can, I grab the suitcase I keep under the bed – it was supposed to be used only if Mama came back to get me in the middle of the night, but there is no better reason than now. It contains only the things I wouldn't want to leave behind. I can't wait for Mama anymore. I tried to hang on, but I need to save myself. It doesn't appear that Mama is going to save me this time. I never go back to that house, and I never see Buddy again.

The walk to Eric's seems to take forever. I am walking slow, in pain. It is dark by the time I get there. I was worried he wouldn't be home, but I see the outside light on and I'm relieved. I make it to the front door and collapse on the top step. I'm safe now. My adrenaline has wore off and I'm suddenly exhausted. Eric has heard me bang against the door and opens it, looking down at me horrified. He gathers me up and gets me into the house, sitting me at the kitchen table. I'm calm, I don't cry. I have no tears to waste on Michael. Eric gets a cold cloth and gingerly dabs at my face; wincing when I wince. He is frantic, asking me what happened. I tell him the truth, and he wants to rush out and find Michael. I calm him down. Going after Michael will only get Eric hurt, and I won't be responsible for that. He wants me to call the police, but I refuse. He tries to convince me, and he's frustrated when I won't change my mind. It's not his fault; he's doing and saying everything he should, he just doesn't understand the world I grew up in - you never involved the police, you handled your own business. Eric is pacing around angrily. I just want to go to sleep.

Later that night when Eric is asleep, I get up the courage to call Daddy's personal number. I don't have Mama right now and I just want a parent. I feel like an orphan, and I just want to hear his voice. After all I've been through tonight, I don't have any fear. I dial the number and it rings and rings. The answering machine picks up and I hear him say, "You've reached Graham. Leave me a message." I don't know what to say. I think I might have quietly said, "Daddy..." before I hang up.

IV:

Life goes on without Mama. I hope she is happy wherever she is. I often wonder if she left because of Michael, now knowing what he is capable of. I wouldn't blame her for that. She has now been gone almost a year. I'm still not panicking yet, because she was gone for a year before when she left me with Uncle Freddie, and she still came back even after that long. Eric says I should seriously consider reporting her missing to the police, but he doesn't understand her. I have told him a bit about my life, but not everything. He doesn't know what she is capable of, and the lengths to which she has gone to make herself vanish, despite the fact that she might cause others to worry. She has no regard for other people's feelings. Plus, I'm an adult now, not a child. She barely had any responsibility to me when I was little, so I'm sure she feels pretty much zero now. I think she is living her life and to hell with the rest of us.

I am staying with Eric now. I have nowhere else to go and he is happy to have me, but it doesn't feel right. I feel like I'm taking advantage of him and his hospitality. I still don't want a relationship. I'm not even sure that I'm capable of loving someone. I'm giving him the wrong idea, giving him hope. I'm so messed up, and he deserves better. His life is stalled, waiting for me. He doesn't date, he doesn't go out with his friends; he's losing himself in me. It breaks my heart, the way he looks at me with so much emotion in his eyes, as if willing me to feel as he feels. I feel like I'm stopping him from living his life. I have a lot of guilt and something needs to change. I either need to get my head on straight or find somewhere else to go and leave him in peace.

I change my mind about involving the police when a year and

a half has gone by without any word from Mama. I don't care if she's happily living her life somewhere, it's not fair of her to do this to me. I want the police to find her, show up at her door, and make her accountable to me. How dare she leave me this way after all I've been through with her; all the years that my life has been put on hold to follow her crazy journey. I'm so mad at her that it eats me up inside. For so long I was not able to be angry. When I was very young, being angry got me ignored at best, otherwise it got me in trouble. As I grew older, I couldn't even feel anger because I could not feel anything. My feelings were ignored for so long, that I became numb. With her missing, everything is coming to the surface, and I need closure. I need to tell her everything that's in my heart: all the ways she has failed me, how she has changed who I am, how much she has hurt me, and let others hurt me. I imagine the confrontation over and over again. For once, she'll have no choice but to listen to me. I can stand up for myself now. I'll finally have my say and I'll be ready.

I go to the police station in person to make the report, sitting with the detective for a long time. He now knows more about my life than anyone, even Eric. So many things were revealed while trying to explain why I have waited so long to report Mama missing. No one waits over a year to report their mother missing, but then again, no one has a mother like Mama.

Detective Killian is skeptical at first. He sits staring at me with hard blue eyes, with the pen held firmly against his notebook. He doesn't start taking me seriously and actually writing notes until I have told him enough so that he understands. I might not be clear on exactly where I was at all times when I was little, but I remember names and a lot of details. I was trying to gather as much information as I could to help Daddy find me. Gathering information was the only thing I could do back then to feel any sense of control over the situation, and I thought that I was helping myself. The more I speak, the more questions the detective has. I tell him the names of all the low life people Mama has been around in the past, and everything that happened to us, and happened to me. By the end, he is looking at me with a look of pity in his face, reminding me why I have never shared my life story with anyone before, and will likely never share these details again.

I feel uncomfortable reporting her as missing. I want to tell him that she is just selfish, and that I might be involving them in a wild goose chase. I want to tell them she is hiding and doesn't want to be found because she has no consideration for anyone else, even her own daughter, but I stick to the facts. He takes all my information and say they will open an investigation immediately and will keep in regular contact with me. He ends the interview saying he call me if they have questions or leads.

I no longer go near the house to check if Mama has returned, but I do keep an eye out for her car around town. I'm not making the effort for her anymore. If she wants to find me, she can come looking for me. I'm not hard to find. I've put in enough time, enough heartache and lord knows, I've waited too many times over the years for her. I'm not waiting anymore. I'm going to live my own life and if she wants to be part of it, she'll have to make the effort. I'd like to say that I've washed my hands of her. I'd like to say that I'm so hardened that I don't even care anymore, but I can't. I can't shut off my feelings. The unfulfilled childhood need for a mother's love and acceptance still burns deep inside me. The lack of a maternal connection has rendered me half a person, forever searching for something to make me whole. It is an emptiness that I have felt for many years and I'm not sure I'll ever be able to repair the damage.

V:

Someone is following me. Over the past week, I have seen the same shiny black car parked in the same spot across the street from Eric's. I notice it when I leave for work and it's still there when I come home. This alone means nothing, but a couple times I have seen it driving down the street slowly behind me as I'm walking to or from the house. Whoever it is hasn't approached me. In fact, if they catch me looking at the car, they drive off or quickly turn onto the nearest street. It's happened too many times, and is too apparent, to be a coincidence. It's always the same car. They stay far enough away that I can't see the driver, but close enough for me to know that I'm not imagining things.

At first, I just thought I was being paranoid, because who would have a reason to follow me around? I wonder if Mama has sent someone to watch over me while she's getting ready to come back and get me. That wouldn't be like her though; she's not subtle. If she wants me, she will plow on in like a bull in a china shop and try to convince me to come away with her. Is she trying to avoid Buddy and Michael while still keeping track of me? My mind runs wild. What could she be involved in now that has resulted in someone following me? I can't imagine, but I drive myself crazy wondering where she is.

A terrifying thought occurs to me. What if this has nothing to do with Mama. What if this is about Stark, and he or his men are trying to find Mama? They aren't just going to forget about the money she stole from them. They are dangerous people and I always had a worry in the back of my mind that they might come looking for us. Both of us know too much. A lot of time has passed, granted, but men like this don't forgive and forget. She probably made a lot of enemies when she took off. She betrayed them, stole their money and knows their secrets. She's not safe, and by extension, neither am I. If they are looking for her and can't find her, maybe they are tailing me thinking I will lead them to her. Maybe that's why she disappeared and hasn't come back. She must be hiding from them – that would make sense. She's hiding until it's safe to come back for me. This brings me a bit of comfort, but is also very concerning. If the person in the black car has something to do with Stark, I am not safe.

I keep this all to myself and try to go on with life as normal. It should be obvious that I haven't seen or spoken to Mama. They must realize that she is nowhere around. They've had plenty of opportunities to approach me and they never have. I debate over whether or not to share this all with Eric, but I decide there's no sense in telling him, I don't want him involved in my mess. However, it is time to seriously consider moving on in order to keep Eric safe. I can't stay in his life – my problems will become his problems. He'll be better off without me, even if he won't agree with me about that. My first inclination is to leave Eric as Mama and I have always left, during the night without another word. Another midnight flight to avoid a confrontation; another bridge burnt. I'm struggling against the urge just to run, but I can't do that to him. It would break his heart, and he deserves better than that, even though he might be better off in the long run if I'm gone. Maybe his career will skyrocket like Daddy's did after I left. If my leaving brings other people good luck, then maybe I've found my worth.

Over the next few days, my head is a very busy place. My thoughts and worries are swirling and my conscience has been bothering me. I am worrying about being followed and what it all means, while trying to figure out how and when to leave Eric. Most importantly, I'm trying to ignore the little voice in my heart that doesn't want me to become Mama. I'm pushing Eric away and it's killing me, but I need to go.

VI:

Thankfully, as fate would have it, I do not have to do anything to Eric that I will regret. My opportunity to run, ironically, is initiated unknowingly by him.

On a warm night in late Spring, he gets a visitor. Jack Kade is rock star in his own right. His band "Shades of Grace" have found a modicum of fame and are soon embarking on their first world tour, after years of putting in their dues around the country. Their hard rock songs and heavy rock ballads are getting a lot of air play. Jack and Eric met at a festival where they both played sets, along with several other bands. Eric also ended up filling in for Jack's bass player on short notice, and they've been friends ever since.

Jack and Eric sit around the roaring fire pit in the yard having a beer, when I come home that night. Eric introduces me as his friend. Jack salutes with a big smile. His long, curly brown hair falls in waves on his shoulders. He's not a big man, slim and only slightly taller than me, wearing a black leather jacket and jeans. I wave and smile, saying hello, on my way in the door. It's been a long day. I'm tired and my ears are ringing from the concert. I only want to get into a nice hot shower and go to bed.

I'm standing at the kitchen counter, eating re-heated take out when I hear Eric yell to me through the open window, "Hey Sunni! Sing that song we wrote together. You know the one."

Of course I know the one. It's the duet he wants me to sing with him on his new album; the offer I declined because I have no desire to be in the spotlight. It's a love song about apologizing for love lost and time gone by.

I don't know why he wants me to sing, but I belt out the female part of the duet, my voice carrying loud and particularly husky tonight after a night of working, and singing along with a concert in a smokey concert hall. I get lost in the music and I'm still singing when Eric shouts again,

"Ok now sing that really popular song by Jack's band. You know the one."

I look quizzically out the window. They are both sitting there looking in at me.

I walk out the backdoor, a fork full of leftovers in one hand and a knife in the other, "What..."

Before I can finish my question, Jack starts singing the lyrics to Shades of Grace's highest rated song, 'Midnight Ride'.

"Well it's midnight, I'm wound tight, I gotta feeling..." He's motioning enthusiastically with his hands for me to join in. So I do, "It's alright...it's right now...and somehow, I'll find you. You can run, but you can't hide...you can run, but don't hide..."

My food falls off my fork onto the ground when I start using the utensils for drum sticks, air drumming as I finish the rest of the chorus. I realize that Jack has stopped singing and he's just listening now. I stop singing.

Jack looks at Eric, and Eric looks back at Jack. They nod at each and lean in close, talking quietly.

I shrug and go back into the house and start eating again, eager to get to the shower.

Eric calls me back out again.

I sigh and give up on my re-heated leftovers, that are now cold again, and throw them in the garbage. I go outside and pull up a chair.

Jack and Eric look at each other again. I shrug questioningly.

"I have a proposition for you," Jack's got a big grin on his face.

Jack goes on to explain that their world tour is set to kick off in the next couple weeks. They are down a crew member. Someone quit suddenly and they are scrambling to fill a position. They need a jack-of-all-trades. The job includes setting up and taking down equipment, and working the lights and the audio equipment. There would also be opportunities to sing back up and generally just be on the road with the band to help during the tour. It would mean travelling with them. I could stop at any leg of the tour I wanted, or I could go on to the end. It's a year long tour, likely more, almost non-stop. They are starting in New York, heading to Europe and ending in London, England. It really is the opportunity of a lifetime.

It doesn't take me much thought. I agree to take the job. This solves everything. I will get away from whoever is following me, trying to find Mama. I can leave Eric to get on with his own life and career, and I don't have to break his heart by leaving him. I will miss Eric, but I can't stand the guilt I have that I might be holding him back, and the urge to has been becoming intolerable. It will also allow me to establish myself further into the music world, increasing my chances of running across Daddy. It couldn't be more perfect.

Jack and I shake on it, and just like that I'm hired. I will sign paperwork before the tour starts.

I go to sleep that night full of nervous excitement about this new chapter of my life. I'm giving up Eric and giving up on Mama, since she won't be able to find me. However, the flip side of the coin - my own life is finally starting. I'm no longer Sunni the little girl who needs saving. I'm shedding that skin and leaving it in the past, and finding my own way. I feel liberated; this is the freedom I've been waiting for, and I'm not looking back.

I:

The one tie I leave to Mama is letting Detective Killian know how to reach me if they find out anything about her; that is the right thing to do. I still need to have it out with her whenever she shows her face. I'm patient and I'll wait as long as it takes. Being away from her all this time has changed me, given me strength. Just like being with her made me weak. As an adult, I'm very much flawed, but I'm now capable of confronting her and the past she created. Little Sunni wasn't able to; she's gone now, but I carry her pain in my heart and I'll make sure she gets redemption.

Eric is tearful when we part. I am sad also, but I can't force tears to come. They just won't anymore. We promise to keep in touch and I make sure he knows that he saved my life and how important he is to me. He says we will run into each other along the way, and I believe this. When drops me off at the tour bus to meet up with the band, he gives me a final hug goodbye, holding on a few extra seconds before reluctantly letting go.

The following days are a whirlwind of excitement, leaving me no time to think about anything other than the tour. I meet the rest of the band: Gib the mysterious dark haired, goatee'd keyboard player who always wears a black cap and sunglasses and speaks very little; Bryce the loud and sarcastic bass guitarist with long curly blonde hair; and Kel, a huge man who almost dwarfs the drum set when he sits at it to play. They welcome me with open arms and it's like having a bunch of brothers adopt me. It is a different kind of family, but feels like family nonetheless. Sometimes the best family, is the one you get to choose for yourself. Especially if your own family is a constant disappointment. I know I made the right choice taking this job, and I haven't been this contented in a long time.

The days are spent travelling non-stop on a big tour bus; we sleep, have impromptu singalongs and play cards as the miles pass. The nights are spent in a rush of activity and music. We'll be flying eventually when we leave the country, but for now, we roll along the highways killing time from venue to venue. When the show is on, I'm racing around behind the scenes taking care of the logistics of putting on a show, troubleshooting problems with equipment, and the whole time I'm singing and smiling – thrilled to be a part of it all.

The first time I am asked to take a place on the stage to sing backup with another girl, I am terrified. I've never sang in front of a crowd before. I prefer my work behind the scenes, out of sight. Jack comes back stage to calm me down, and it makes me feel better by telling me that all eyes will be on him as the singer, and I just need to sing and forget about everything else. I have been through more difficult things in my life, so I get up on that stage. It is lit up enough that the audience is just a dark blur; I don't think about them, I just sing. I let myself get lost in the music and soon I'm enjoying myself. Being a part of something so big is exhilarating. The audience is clapping and cheering. I feel at home.

As the weeks fly by, I watch Eric's star rising. His band's first album is released and they are getting a lot of air play on the radio stations. Their first single charts well and is climbing. I'm so proud of him. I make time to call him and it feels good to hear his voice. He lets me know that there is no news about Mama, but he's keeping an eye out. He also tells me that he has a girlfriend. This makes me feel...something...maybe it's jealousy. I don't want to share Eric, but I can't keep him, so I have to let him go. I swallow the lump in my throat and tell him I'm happy for him. He tells me to keep in touch and when we hang up, I hold onto the receiver for a long time before I put it in the cradle.

Jack and I have become close; a relationship that has been slowly building since the tour started. He's fun to be around and he makes me laugh. I thought something was happening between us, but I wasn't sure until the night there was a party in his hotel room to celebrate the last show on the Eastern leg of the tour. It raged on late into the night, until people started leaving one by one. Finally, it was just him and I left in his room, and we talked a blue streak into the wee hours of the morning, and made plans to write songs together. He didn't want me to leave his room that night, and we've been together ever since.

We do write songs together, and it's like magic. Everything comes together brilliantly - my lyrics, his music. I'm still in love with the process of watching our art come to life. Words put to music are a beautiful thing, and the best therapy for easing a troubled mind. Our songs are sung night after night in concert, and the audience loves them. They top the charts when they're released as singles. The more popular the band becomes, the more money rolls in. We are flying high, drunk on our own creative power. At this moment in time, we are invincible.

The paparazzi catches wind of Jack's new relationship and pictures of us end up in magazines with reporters, and by extension the public, wondering who Jack's new girlfriend is. Jack, the beloved lead singer of "Shades of Grace" has a girlfriend, and the world goes crazy. I'm not used of people caring who I am. Our picture is taken constantly, everywhere we are there are cameras in our faces. We wear dark glasses and start sneaking in and out of back doors, surrounded by security. After awhile they stop caring and the fuss dies down. This is a strange existence.

This is my first real grown up relationship; an actual relationship, as opposed to the meaningless time I've killed with other guys to keep from going home. I haven't had a good role model to show me what a relationship is supposed to look like or what love is supposed to be. There's no one I can ask questions to or confide in. I don't want to appear like I'm in over my head, but I don't really know how to be part of a couple. I don't know what to do or how to act. I just dive in blindly, and I'm winging it the best I can. Jack is older than me by 12 years, which makes some people, especially management, shake their heads at us. We don't care what people think – we're just living life and enjoying this time together. We are young, crazy and in love.

Daily though, I fight a battle between my heart and my head – my heart wants to love recklessly and without forethought, while my head keeps telling me that I don't deserve love...that I need to keep space between Jack and I...that I need to push him away like I did to Eric. It helps that we are in the midst of exceptional circumstances – trapped together travelling around on a tour bus, living the rock star life. It is easier to love this way because this isn't real life. I don't know if it's even real love. So for now, I can pretend to be normal and quit listening to that dysfunctional little voice that seeks to destroy my happiness.

II:

Autumn rolls around and we are on the Western leg of the tour, a few shows still to come in the North and then we'll be off to Europe and finally England. It's an exhausting life, and in some ways, similar to life when I was young – living out of suitcases, always travelling, sleeping in different places, never staying anywhere too long. The irony is not lost on me. My life seems to have come around full circle.

I wonder where Mama is living, how she is living, and who is she living with. I hope she is being treated well, but I know that she is her own worst enemy and her circumstances likely haven't improved. Although I like to picture her living well, finally finding somewhere she feels at home, the more likely scenario is that she is still bouncing around from place to place and person to person. She most certainly is still living the same hand to mouth existence. Life could have been different for Mama, but she doesn't know any other way. She doesn't see choices or opportunities or a different path. She will always take the hard way. I think of her often, but not every day. If I think too much, I will lose my mind. I have to leave her in the past, until I'm able to deal with her in the present. I wonder if she ever thinks about me.

It happened after a particularly gruelling show before we started North, and it happened completely unexpectedly. Nothing could have prepared me for it.

I was called by the tour manager who told me I had a phone call. My mind starts racing. I wonder who would be tracking me down on the road. Maybe Mama had returned and Eric was calling to let me know that she was looking for me. Well, she isn't going to find me this time. I'm no longer joining Mama on her crazy journey. I'm 20 years old now, and I certainly will not be running back to Mama. Maybe Eric gave her my contact information and Mama is calling herself and we are going to have that conversation right now over the phone. I hold the receiver, take a deep breath and prepare what I'm going to say before I take the call. Everything that has been bottled up deep inside is going to come out; all the imaginary confrontations that I've practiced over and over in my head late at night when I can't sleep. My heart is hard when I say hello. I'm ready for this.

But I'm not ready for the deep voice from the past that says, "Sunni? Sunni is it you?"

"Daddy...", it comes out as a whimper and I sink into the chair beside the phone.

The sun is setting and the hotel room is getting dark. I look over to make sure the door is locked, and I don't turn on the light. All the air has gone out of me and I can't breathe. For the first time in a long time, I can feel all my emotions again. I feel everything all at once...tears are running down my face. I'm sniffling and quietly sobbing, and I can barely put two words together.

"Sunni, my God I've finally found you. Where have you been all this time?" Daddy is crying too.

"Daddy why didn't you come and get me? Why didn't you find me?"

Suddenly I'm 8 years old again. I'm the little girl who wished and prayed, and talked to the sky waiting for her Daddy to come and save her.

"Sunni, girl, I've been looking for you since the moment your Mama took you out the door. I couldn't find hide nor hair of either of you, until recently." Daddy's voice is comforting and familiar, and the world is right again.

"We've been so many places. Mama had us moving constantly. I missed you so much. I just wanted to go home." My voice is barely above a whisper and my eyes are blind with tears.

"Oh Sunni, when I couldn't find you myself, I hired a private detective. Every time we'd get close to finding you, we had just missed you. You were gone again. We'd lose track of you for months at time and then you'd turn up briefly and be gone again. We've been looking for so long. I thought I'd never see you again." Daddy sniffs and clears his throat. He's done crying now.

Daddy goes on to explain that he was finally able to track me down once I took a job in the business. Daddy had many contacts and acquaintances in the music world; people talk, and it came back to him that I was working on a concert at one of the venues he had also played at. It ended up paying off that I kept telling people that my Daddy was Graham Sage. It was a fluke, a sheer fluke, that made this happen. I made this happen.

Daddy says that his private detective had discovered the town we were living in, when Mama married Buddy. He was able to find Buddy's house, but by then I was staying with Eric, so he lost me again. It took him a bit, but he found me at Eric's, and Daddy says the detective trailed me for awhile to make sure he had found the right person, before reporting back to Daddy. Then I disappeared again – going on tour with Jack.

I have to laugh when he says that, and tell him that I'm so glad that's who was following me because I thought for sure it was Stark, and this leads to a long discussion about how my time was spent in those missing years. I end up telling Daddy of the long and exhausting, traumatizing journey that Mama took me on after we left him. I tell him of the nights spent in the car, in dingy motels, with strangers, with strange men...I tell him of being scared and hungry and alone...of being neglected and lonely and abandoned over and over again. I tell him almost everything...almost...because I don't think he can handle anymore. He's crying again, and telling me over and over again how sorry he is that he couldn't find me and how guilty he feels. We cry together; we talk for a long time. The years melted away, but they are still lost forever.

I tell him about being in the audience at his concert, and calling and hanging up on his phone. He tells me of countless hours spent pouring over maps and documents and seeking legal advice and getting nowhere. Finally he asks about Mama, and I tell him that I haven't heard from her in over two years now, and that I have reported her missing. He confirms that his detective also lost her trail after she married Buddy. Wherever she is now, we both agree that she doesn't want to be found. He suggests that she might not even be in the country anymore. She always talked about wanting to move far away; she had dreams of living in Italy or France, he says. She was always a dreamer, always wanting more than she had. To her, the grass was always greener somewhere else. He felt like he could never make her happy.

Daddy sighs, and his reminiscing about Mama is over. He tells me that he is about to go back on tour, so he won't be available to meet for awhile due to his contractual obligations. I tell him about Jack and that we are also on tour. He bristles a little at the mention of Jack, and me being his girlfriend. I get the distinct impression that he doesn't like Jack, but he doesn't say anything. We compare venues to see if we're going to be anywhere close, but we aren't. Our long awaited reunion will have to wait even longer, but I have my Daddy in my life again – after over 10 years of wasted time. My heart is so full when we finally hang up. We are going to keep in touch and talk as much as we can until the day that we can see each other face to face...and what a beautiful reunion that will be.

III:

It seems cruel that when one part of my life is finally

satisfied, another part starts to fail. Jack and I have been fighting a lot. Truth be told, we are both immature – me trying to navigate my first real relationship with no idea how, and Jack being an overgrown child, despite his age. We fight over silly things, we make up quickly and then fight again. Our latest fight was when Jack wrote a song about our relationship, telling our secrets to the world. He says it's going to be a big hit. I hope it never gets released. Our fights are intense; our making up is intense. It is a vicious cycle, and I think living and working with each other all day, every day is starting to wear on us.

The novelty of the road is wearing off; the days are long and the routine is monotonous. Birthdays and holidays are celebrated on the road, we lose track of the days and the places we've been. The band, my group of adopted brothers, are starting to get on my nerves with their constant presence, and their stupid jokes and tricks. At the end of the day though, it still comes together beautifully on stage and we still produce show after show flawlessly. The reviews in the news and music magazines are good and "Shades of Grace" and their music is more popular then ever. The band is a money making machine for everyone involved. No one wants to stop the cash flow, especially management. So we keep going; show after show, city after city. It is an exhausting pace, full of chaos, and it's starting to remind me too much of life with

Mama.

I have lost track of Eric. I haven't talked to him in a long time. He's still riding his wave of success, touring and releasing more singles. I follow his career, as I follow Daddy's. I want to tell Eric that I've found Daddy and have reconnected with him, but I'm never able to reach him. He's busy now and doesn't seem to have time for me. I guess I've lost him, and I do feel the twinges of regret – more water under the bridge. I miss him.

I call Detective Killian, just once, to check on the investigation. They haven't been able to find out anything. Mama's vanishing act is a good one this time. I ask him if it possible that she might have left the country, and he admits that is something to consider, and will definitely make the investigation a little more difficult. He reassures me that they are still working on it, looking for leads and talking to a lot of people. Even though most of the people have nothing to say and won't give up any information, he tells me not to lose hope. I am leaving it in his hands. I can't let my head fill up with worries and theories. I won't give her anymore of my time, physically or mentally. She left me on my own, so now I'm returning the favour. I keep saying that, but I'm still compelled to keep checking in.

I manage to talk to Daddy one more time, very briefly, two or three months after our first call. He is very difficult to reach. It's not enough. I need more of him, more of his time. He has over 10 years to make up for. I need him to be there when I need to talk to him. Maybe it's selfish, but I don't care. I've waited so long, it's my turn now. He says he wants me to visit him some day, at the old house that I lived in until I didn't. I can't do that. I can't walk back into that place full of memories and see someone else living there and calling my family, my house, their own. I have no interest in meeting his wife or his stepsons. I don't tell him that, but I know that it's never going to happen.

It is an awkward call that ends on a bit of a sour note, when he tells me that he wouldn't have wished life in the music world for me. He wishes I had not followed his path. He says there are too many dangers, too many untrustworthy people, he doesn't want me to get hurt. After being absent for more years of my life than he was present, he has no right to give me any sort of advice. I'm a bit indignant. It's too late to parent me now. I know I'm angry at Mama, but I never realized how angry I also am at Daddy, and that takes me by surprise. For years I have ached for the day that we'd find each other again. I guess I built it up so much in my head – the only thing I needed was my Daddy and then everything would be perfect, but I'm quickly finding out it's not going to be that easy. There is not going to be a fairy tale ending.

We are now on a flight to Europe. It's a long flight, and we are all restless. I am happy to be off the bus, but I'm still feeling like a caged animal, trapped in never ending chaos. Life won't slow down so I can take a moment and just breathe. I haven't had any time to rest my body or my mind in a long time. I need time to recover from my childhood, to process reconnecting with Daddy, to figure out how to live without Mama, and just to be a normal human being...

We have several shows in Europe, and then some in England, and finally the tour will be done. I have signed on for the final leg of the tour so I'm stuck until the bitter end. Jack and I have a terrible fight on the plane before we land. It's a fight over nothing really – just the drama of two immature people living a rock star life, with no concept of the real world. Everything on the road is amplified, every disagreement seems huge. I need a change of scenery. I will not quit the tour, but I need something more.

The tour manager connects me with some of his European contacts. I get some work doing demo recordings and background vocals for some European bands. It helps to get away from Jack and the band and try something new. It eases my mind and keeps me sane. I'm offered my own representation there, and although it would be the stepping stone to fame, I'm still not interested in being in the spot light, front and centre. I'm content to stay in the background. A lot of people would jump at the opportunity, but it doesn't appeal to me. I don't need to see my name in lights. I have crossed paths with too many people in my short life, and I don't need them to come crawling out of the woodwork if I were to become famous. They each stole a little piece of my childhood and I will not give them anymore. My desire for peace and privacy trumps my desire for fame and fortune.

I try to keep in touch with Daddy, but I've been unable to reach him. I know he's busy and touring, but I really need someone. I feel like I have no one. With Mama gone, Eric living a life apart from me, Jack being...Jack, I feel very isolated, even though I'm around people all day, every day. My soul can feel that something is wrong, and struggles to right itself. I don't know the answer, but I know something has to change.

We continue to do show after show, singing the same songs night after night. All in all, Europe has been a big success. Jack is a brilliant showman, and he's having the time of his life, riding his wave of fame. He's a ball of energy, a spitfire, he never slows down – running around that stage every night from one end to the other. He lives life at a frenetic pace, forcing me to keep up or get left behind. He's always moving, always has to be busy; he doesn't know how to relax. The cheering crowds seem to be his fuel. They love Jack...and the girls love Jack...and Jack loves the girls. He flirts with them, fights with me. I'm not jealous – like always, I am numb. I know he loves me in his own way, he tells me all the time. I say it back, but I don't even know what love feels like. I'm going through the motions, but I'm not even sure how or why. I can feel myself pulling away slowly, and it scares me.

IV:

Finally we reach England, and the people welcome us with open arms. They go crazy over Jack. He entertains the crowds with the same energy and enthusiasm every night, even though the rest of us are starting to slow down. We are exhausted and ready for it to all be over. England is where everything starts to go wrong.

The other guys are becoming jealous of the spotlight always being on Jack, instead of the entire band. Jack is constantly referred to as the front man, even though he continually says that he is not the front man, only the lead singer. There's a big fight one night when a local tv show is only interested in interviewing Jack and not all of them. He is eclipsing the rest of the band, and his ego is growing every day; so is the animosity. Punches are actually thrown, things are said that cannot be unsaid. The tour manager has to cancel a few shows. Kel and Bryce threaten to quit. The tension among them is awful.

With the threat of being sued for not meeting their contractual obligations, their manager tells them, in no uncertain terms, to get themselves together and finish this tour. So they do, but it's no longer fun for anyone. The band is imploding from within. It's sad to watch, but it's inevitable. The last three shows were gruelling and not up to par, as they are struggling to keep it together. They don't socialize after the shows anymore, there are no more parties. They go back to their own rooms and just wait to be done.

At night, I lay beside Jack feeling a million miles away from him. We are actually getting along well these past weeks. He's leaning on me for support; he wants it to be us against them, but I'm not that invested. Whatever happens to the band, Jack will go on with or without them. He's poised and ready for a solo career. He will be just fine.

After the last show, Jack and I sit in the motel room alone. I tell him I need to leave. I can't do this anymore. I can't follow his dreams, and he can't stop following them – I would never ask him to. He asks me to reconsider, to stay with him, but I tell him no. He's heartbroken, but he's not completely surprised. The last few months have been difficult. We still love each other, we just can't make it work under these circumstances. We say goodbye tenderly, spending one last night together. I don't know how I can leave Jack so easily, but I've always been able to turn off my emotions and push my feelings so far away so that I become numb. It scares me.

I don't wait to fly home with the band. I catch a flight the very next morning back home alone. Jack brings me to the airport and we hug warmly and wish each other well. He turns around and walks away with his hands in his pockets of his jeans and his head hanging down. I watch him for only a moment, wondering if I'm doing the right thing. It would be so easy to run after him and continue this life; change is terrifying. But that wouldn't be fair to me. I have to let him go and move on. I have no idea where my life is heading right now, or how I'm going to start over, but I owe it to myself. I owe it to the little girl who is finally getting a chance to find her own way.

I find out later that Jack has written a song about our breakup. Once again, he shares our private moments with the world, pouring out his emotions in song, with little regard for my feelings. People can now sing along about the demise of our relationship. I don't really know how I feel about that. It's a sad ballad, just his voice and his guitar, and it's an instant hit. One verse in particular tugs at my heart. He sings, "I wish she wouldn't go, because she doesn't know, how much she is loved." Every time I hear the song on the radio, I will always be reminded of this time in my life when Jack was my world.

I:

Although I've told myself all the way home that I won't, the first thing I do is drive by Buddy's house to see if Mama's car is there. Of course it isn't. I let Detective Killian know that I'm back in town, and he tells me they haven't been able to find Mama yet, as I expected. Eric is busy travelling and playing music and has subleased his house out to a friend, which I find out when I stop by to let him know that I'm back. So, I'm staying at a motel until I get myself sorted out. I have nowhere else to go. I'm alone... I'm so alone.

I want Daddy to know where to find me, I want him to talk to me, but all I can do is leave a message and hope he calls me back. He's overseas and communication is not good. This is the biggest tour of his career. Some are wondering if it's a farewell tour, but he hasn't confirmed that to the public. The rumour in the music world is that he might be taking an extended break after this tour. I know only as much as the rest of the world does, and nothing more. I'm an outsider in his life.

The money from being on the road for so long has allowed me to get myself a little car and rent a small apartment above a bakery in the middle of town. I don't like being alone. I was alone far too long as a child, but at the same time, I embrace it. I need time to know who I am without Mama, without a man... just me. I'm trying, but I don't even know where to begin.

I get in touch with the company I used to work for before I left town, and they hire me back. So I'm back on the local circuit, working on local concerts again. I spend my days keeping as busy as I can, trying to avoid my own thoughts and fears. At night, I go back to my empty apartment and sit in silence. Sometimes I stare at the phone, wishing and praying for Daddy to call. I sleep restlessly, in bits and pieces, lying awake watching the hours tick by. Then I get up and do it all over again the next day. The life I have now is a stark contrast to the loud craziness of being on tour. I often look through the decorative box of Polaroids, news clippings, snippets of songs and other mementos I kept from my time with Jack. I miss him, but I don't know if I miss Jack himself, or if I miss being part of something. Maybe I need to live in chaos. Maybe I don't know any other way. I put the box on a high shelf in the bedroom closet, underneath a bunch of other boxes and leave it there. I won't look at it again.

I have men asking me out, but I'm not interested in getting into another relationship. I can't get on that roller coaster again so soon. I don't have the energy to get to know someone, and I have no desire to let anyone know me. I'm done telling my story. Months go by and my mind doesn't change. However, backstage at a concert one night, I meet Kip. He's an aspiring musician, playing guitar and singing backup for the headlining band that night. He has big dreams of becoming a lead singer and having his own band. He wears the stereotypical leather jacket, has the prerequisite long hair, the killer smile of musician, and girls throwing themselves at him. I've seen it all before.

At first, I dismiss Kip like all the rest of them, but I begin to see that he is different. Kip is so focused on himself, that he isn't looking for a relationship either. He isn't interested in an emotional connection and he isn't asking anything of me besides my time and companionship. I start hanging out with him casually; he is someone I can be intimate with, who doesn't expect anything else from me. It allows me a freedom I've never known before. I don't have to surrender my soul, no emotional investment, nothing deep and meaningful. I don't have to think. We play sports, joining a baseball team together and travelling to the games. We watch baseball and football games on tv or attend them in person. I was never much for sports, but Kip's enthusiasm for anything competitive is contagious and I find myself enjoying it. I purposely root for different teams than him and we enjoy a friendly rivalry. We watch movies and talk about them. We go on road trips, and run errands together. We talk about books, the universe, music... anything but anything serious. He doesn't care who my Daddy is. He doesn't ask me a million questions about my life. It is just what I need, a friend with no commitment. He gets me out of my head and into enjoying life again. I'm not sitting alone at home in silence anymore. He doesn't even have a clue how good he is for me. He uses me and I use him – and it works wonderfully.

II:

I'd like to think that I could live the rest of my life in this non-committal state, but fate has other plans. It's been months since I've been hanging out with Kip and I feel more alive than I've felt in a long time.

I'm sitting backstage, cross-legged on the ground surrounded by wires, trying to determine where the malfunction is in a soundboard. I've got a wire in one hand and a puzzled look on my face. I'm so focused on what I'm doing, that I don't even hear him walk up to me, until he says, "Well, hi stranger."

I look up, squinting in concentration, then I drop the wire and jump to my feet excitedly, "Eric!"

Without thinking, I throw my arms around him and hug him tight. I'm so happy to see him. He's cut his hair short, and he looks a little older, and I can't stop staring at him. I let him go and look around, in case his girlfriend is there.

"Sunni! So good to see you. I heard you were here and thought I'd come see for myself." He's smiling, the impish grin that I've missed so much.

"It's been a long time. How are you? You're looking good." I tell him.

"I'm really good. Things are really good. Just got back into town. Been on the road a long time, so I'm looking forward to the break. Taking a breather for awhile and then going back into the studio to make album number two." He leans forward and says quietly, "I've missed you."

"I missed you too." It's the truth. I hug him again. "Oh sorry, I shouldn't be all over you like this. Is your girlfriend here with you?"

"I don't have a girlfriend."

We go out for dinner that night, and we have so much to say to each other. He's surprised when I tell him about Daddy, and wishes he could have been there for me. He's sorry that there's been no word about Mama yet, but he thinks she knows exactly what she's doing. When she does turn up, he says I should give her a piece of my mind. Don't worry, I say, I've been practicing for that very moment for a long time, and I'm looking forward to it.

We share stories of being on tour. He had heard that Jack and I were together and he admits that he purposely didn't call me back because he didn't want to interfere, so he kept his distance. He tells me his experiences on the road, although his tour was on a much smaller scale than Jack's band. We talk and talk; there is so much to catch up on. The night is getting later and later.

He wants to show me his new house. He's bought an ocean front home in a private spot outside of town. As we pull up, it's bathed in moonlight and it's beautiful. The large beach house has a huge front porch running the length of the house, and a second floor balcony, with upper turrets on each side. He opens the heavy wooden front door revealing a huge stone fireplace in the living room. In the open concept living room/dining room there are brown leather couches and a big wooden table and chairs. Floor to ceiling windows let the moonlight in. I congratulate him on his success. This is a far cry from the little place he used to have. He shrugs sheepishly. He pours us a drink and we sit in front of the fire place. We just keeping talking, never running out of things to say. He kisses me and it seems like the most natural thing in the world. I spend the night. We aren't just friends anymore.

Just like that, we are in a relationship. It happens quickly, but it also took forever. The familiarity is comforting. He knows me, he knows my life, what I've let him know anyway, and he accepts me despite it all. There is no pretending, no worries, just relief that we've found our way back to each other. Shortly after, I give up my little apartment and move in with him. It seems fast, but it's not unexpected, we've just been on hold. Whatever I was hesitant about before, whatever made me afraid, is gone. I need him now, and the next time Kip calls, I let him know it's over. He's fine with that, he was never attached.

Eric and I settle into a comfortable life. We are never apart for very long at a time. It's like we are an extension of one another. We laugh, we sing, we love...and I'm happy. It's a good life. It feels right.

I leave my new contact information with Daddy's manager and with Detective Killian. I can't believe how much time has passed without Mama. Maybe this is the best thing she's ever done for me – leave me alone. Maybe this is a gift she doesn't know she gave me. Her selfish abandonment has allowed me to figure out that I can live without her, that I am my own person. I don't have to yearn for her approval anymore. It doesn't matter what she thinks or where she is, I will be fine. She can live her life without the burden of her child. Maybe she also thought she needed me, but realized that she didn't. I will find her one day, and when I do, she'll regret everything she put me through.

Daddy has finally called me. His tour is over and he's back at home. I tell him about Eric, and he begrudgingly accepts that I'm still in the music world. He wants to make plans to get together. I'm nervous and excited, although still harbouring some anger. He wants Eric and I to fly out to see him, but I refuse. I don't tell him that I have no desire to meet his family because I don't want to be rude. Maybe it's selfish on my part, but I need to keep my relationship with Daddy separate and to myself. I ask him to fly here instead to visit with me. He doesn't understand the difference, but he is taking an extended time off, so he agrees to come to the East Coast, and I'm very grateful when he says he's coming alone.

When I finally see Daddy in person, it's mid-summer. The air is heavy and warm, with days of endless blue skies. Daddy flies in from Missouri, rents a car and shows up at our house – just as easy as that. After what feels like a hundred years, I watch as Daddy pulls in the driveway. Eric is standing at the window with me, an arm around my shoulders. I'm shaking and my heart is pounding. I watch him park the car and get out, gathering up his bag and his guitar case. He looks up at the house. There he is. This is the moment I've dreamed of since I was taken out the house over 15 years ago. I feel like I can't move, I can only stare at him. It's like a dream happening right before my eyes.

Eric nudges me towards the door, as Daddy is walking up the driveway. Suddenly I can't get there fast enough. I run out the door, down the front stairs and down the driveway. Tears are threatening to spill and blurring my vision, as I run into his embrace. He picks me up and spins me around. His eyes are also filled with tears.

"Sunni, girl... I thought this day would never come. I thought I'd lost you forever all those years ago." He finally lets me go, and stands back.

"I've always been out here Daddy, waiting for you."

He's older, his hair and beard are greyer, and he's a bit heavier, but he's still the only Daddy I've ever known. My heart is bursting with happiness, but also there's also sadness for all the wasted years gone by. I wipe my eyes, as Daddy shakes Eric's hand and Eric leads us all into the house.

III:

Daddy is only able to stay for a few days. He has family obligations on his time off. He begs me to go back with him and meet everyone, but I decline as graciously as I can. This is enough for me – just having my Daddy here. I don't want anymore. I don't want anyone else. I'm not interested in going back to revisit the past, seeing the house and the room I was taken from, and pretending to be happy that Daddy's life continued as if I had never been there.

The first evening, we sit in front of the fireplace and we talk quietly. Eric has long since gone to bed. Daddy smiles, reminiscing about good times when I was little. He tells me how proud and happy he was when I was born, bragging to anyone who would listen, until his band mates got tired of hearing my name. He and Mama were young and in love, and life was perfect, so he thought. He had a hard time leaving his new baby to go out on the road, but his career was starting to take off and he couldn't ignore his obligations to so many people depending on him. My song, "Sunni, Honey" he says, was written about the struggle he was going through when I was little, wanting to be home, but needing to be gone.

I tell him of life with Mama alone, while he was on the road. I tell him some truths he doesn't want to hear. He didn't know how neglectful Mama was. The house was always clean when he came home, I was fed and seemed to be fine, so he never guessed that anything could be wrong. He admits that he was caught up in his music to the point where he probably overlooked a lot of things, but he trusted Mama to be a good Mama. He had no idea how I was suffering in his absence. He didn't know that I was fed only because I fed myself while Mama lay in bed all day or, alternately, had a house full of company. Whether he wanted to hear it or not, I tell him of Mama leaving me alone and being gone all night; of Mama always having other men hanging around, sitting on their laps, giggling and flirting. I don't want to hurt him with the details, but I need him to know. I need to justify my childhood pain. I need him to understand, and realize that he has some responsibility for it also. I want him to feel guilty. I want him to apologize, because Mama never will.

I don't want our entire visit to be emotional and sad, so the next day Eric and I take Daddy out and show him around. Daddy gets recognized despite his hat and dark glasses. He amiably signs autographs for fans throughout the day. He poses for pictures while we are out for lunch at a local restaurant. Eric gets recognized too. It is the life of a rock a star. I understand it, but my time with Daddy is fleeting and I don't want to share him with anyone. People fawn over Daddy and Eric when we are in public. I am just background noise, glanced at and overlooked. I'm no one important, no one special to them. They don't realize that my story is pivotal to the whole damn thing, and it would be the most heartbreaking to tell. Paparazzi have found out that Daddy is in town, and when they start to follow us, snapping pictures, we make our exit and go back home. I have no doubt we will find ourselves in the papers tomorrow, as they struggle to determine what Daddy's connection is to this town and to the mysterious girl in the photo.

Daddy tells me all about his wife Marie and her sons. I listen quietly and politely, but I don't encourage him and I don't ask questions. They met when she was hired as a back up singer many years ago. Eventually the loneliness of the road brought them together, as they spent more time with each other than they did with their families. He says he gets along well with her sons, one is going through med school and the other just graduated law school. He shows me pictures and tells me stories. It sounds like he has a wonderful life. Marie sounds like a very nice person, but obviously Daddy has been fooled before, so I don't take his word as gospel. I don't want to like her. It hurts to know that he is so happy, but of course, I wouldn't want him to be miserable. My feelings are mixed up and confusing to me. I'm trying not to get lost in them, so I can just live in the moment, but there's no denying that it's not all roses and butterflies. He tells me that he told Marie about me right from the start, and this warms my heart. He says she would love to meet me, and I say sure some day, but I don't mean it. It would be like meeting the Mama I should have had, and that would hurt.

That evening, we sit on beach chairs in the sand, in front of the ocean, listening to the waves crash. The sun is going down; Eric has built a fire. It's been a day full of emotions and talking and feeling, and I'm mentally exhausted. Eric can see that it's difficult, and he lightens the mood by pulling out his guitar. Daddy goes and gets his, saying he never goes anywhere without it. He's always struck by inspiration, and songs can come out of nowhere. I think he's going to have a lot of material to use from this trip. Eric and Daddy sing and play around the fire – their own hits, covers of old songs, anything and everything. It's beautiful to listen to. It's perfect. I join in singing and forget all the rest of it for awhile.

Early the next morning over coffee, Daddy surprises me by giving me a couple names of men that he thinks could be my biological father, which I tuck away in the corner of mind for another time. There's too much going on right now to open yet another can of worms, and I don't have the mental energy to deal with any of that right now. I am curious, but another part of me doesn't even want to know. Daddy says he suspected that Mama was anything but faithful before I was born and when I was younger, but he loved her and he loved being a father, and he was just content to live in denial. However, the time came when he demanded a paternity test, which she put off for a very long time and then hid the results. It was the beginning of the end, and I was caught in the crossfire. In retrospect, he says he feels guilty, and should have just left well enough alone, but we both agree that it would have just delayed the inevitable. Mama would have made our world implode anyway, sooner or later.

Our last day together - it comes so fast. We are trying to cram so much into such a short time, racing against the clock, trying to make up for many lost years. I'm just glad that I was able to make him understand what Mama put me through. He can barely believe the stories I tell him. There aren't even enough words to explain every life I lived as a child – and it does feel like a hundred different lifetimes. I do feel some redemption when Daddy gives me a heartfelt apology after I quietly admit that I'm angry at him too. It helps, but it doesn't change the past, it doesn't make it all better. I thought it would, but I now I know that words can't fix anything.

We spend so much time talking about Mama, as she was pivotal in changing the course of both our lives. We've both been deeply affected by her actions. Now that she's missing, we only have each other to try and work through the mess she's left. Daddy admits his anger at her used to drive him crazy. He was so mad at her for taking me away that it sent him into a downward spiral. He tried to drown his sorrows in booze for several years, but when it threatened his career, he had to let it go and save himself. He says wherever Mama is, she is better off to just stay there - stay gone - he says I am better off without her. I do agree, I've thrived without her, but I tell him that I need to confront her. I feel like I am stuck in a prison of my own making until I can talk to her face to face and let her know how I feel about everything. I didn't have a voice when I was a child. She could brush me off and refuse to listen to me then, but I have a voice now, and I'm going to be heard. He understands this, and he hopes I will get the closure I'm looking for. I know that I will. It's coming. She can't stay hidden forever.

At the airport, I hold onto Daddy long and tight for one last hug. I need to memorize everything about him. I don't want to let go. Eric has been my pillar of strength these past few days, and I collapse into his arms when Daddy's flight takes off. I don't know when I will see him again, and that unknown fills me with fear and sadness. Three days was not enough. At that moment, I finally realize with certainty that it will never be enough – time is just gone.

IV:

After Daddy leaves, life goes on as usual, as though something monumental in my life didn't just happen. Now that it's over, I can't seem to shake the melancholy feeling that has settled over me. I spent so many years hanging onto hope and imagining the perfect ending to my story with Daddy. It's how I put myself to sleep at night when I was young. It's how I settled my troubled mind when I was older. I don't have that to hold onto anymore. It didn't provide me with the happiness or closure I was looking for. In the end, he goes back home to his life and I continue mine. Life, and it's complications, has made sure we will never pick up where we left off. We can only create a new relationship, but I will always yearn for the old one. I will always be a little girl missing her Daddy.

My anguish spills out all over Eric. I'm moody and cranky, and he tries his best to understand. So I also feel guilty that I can't be what Eric needs right now. I'm just hurting and mad at the world. I didn't expect to feel this way after getting the thing I wanted most in the world. It's just too late to heal the poor little girl I was. The woman I have become is angry.

I'm distracted at work, but keeping busy is the best thing I can do. Eventually, after some time passes, my anger is muted, and pushed back into that little box inside my heart with all the other upsets in my life. Eric is happy that I'm acting more like myself, but now it does feels like an act. I do love him so much, but I'm starting to feel inadequate, unfulfilled. I worry that Mama's flight response is in my very DNA.

A few months pass since Daddy's visit, and Eric and I have been together now for a few years. He is wonderful. I can't say a bad word about him. He's constant and consistent. We are fine, life is fine, but something is gnawing in the back of my mind, something making me squirm in my own skin. I've been trying to ignore it and pretend it doesn't exist. I've been waiting for my mind to clear, but I feel like I'm fighting a losing battle.

Eric has another cross country tour looming, and he wants me to come on the road with him. He tries to convince me, but I can't imagine the chaos of touring again. I don't have it in me. He has started to talk about getting married. He doesn't ask me, he hasn't gotten a ring, but he's testing the waters. Maybe he thinks it will make me happy, make me feel better, calm my restless soul after Daddy's emotional visit. He wants us to be together forever. This is a thought I find stifling. The mundane of everyday life is killing me. The funny thing is that he is offering me the very thing that I have been craving since childhood – a stable, normal life. I want it so badly, yet something inside me pushes it away. What is wrong with me? I don't know how to live a regular life. I only know how to run...I need to escape. I *need* to run.

The more he talks about getting married, the more pressured I feel. I don't know how to be what he wants me to be. He talks about having children. What would I, of all people, have to offer a child? I cannot be a mother, if I was never mothered. I'm not going to be responsible for screwing up a child's life and creating another dysfunctional human being. If this is what Eric wants, he's better off to find someone else who can give it to him freely and without reservations. I can't marry Eric and pretend to live a life he wants to live. He wants more from me than I can give, and he deserves so much better. As much as it hurts me, I have to let him go...again.

He begs and pleads with me. He cries. It's for the best...it's for him, why can't he understand that? I know I'm hurting him, but I don't see any other option. I love him, that's why I'm setting him free. There's something wrong with me. I'm breaking my own heart. His tour starts in a few days, and he finally gets that he will be going alone.

I:

I'm starting over again. I'm used to recreating myself, it's the only constant in my life. I'm putting life with Eric behind me. It hurts to think about, so I don't. So many regrets....second guessing myself... how dare Mama turn me into this.

I've moved out of town to the closest big city, a couple hours away. It is a popular concert venue and a big music city, so I find work easily. I'm no longer road crew, but I'm still behind the scenes. I'm learning production, and when I'm not working the soundboards and recording equipment, I'm doing a lot of demo work. I get to sing the written, but unrecorded songs, so that artists, managers, producers can hear what they are supposed to sound like when they are looking for their next big hit. I'm also able to write my own songs for contention. It is a thrill when an artist picks a song you wrote and makes it a hit. The money is rolling in again.

I call Detective Killian to give him the phone number at the small condo I've rented in the music district. We have a lengthy, frank discussion and he tells me that Mama's case has officially gone cold. There are no more leads and no more people to talk to. They aren't closing the case, it will remain open, but there is no longer anything to follow up on. We have to sit and wait now for something to happen; either Mama turns up or someone talks. They did not get a lot of cooperation from anyone they spoke to, which was not surprising. They followed every trail to a dead end. For now.

Detective Killian tells me to never give up hope – cases are solved and people are found after decades. He also says the people that hide the best are the ones that don't ever want to be found. His professional opinion is that, given her history, she has changed her name, adopted a new identity, whether it be false or stolen from someone else, and has no intention of making contact ever again. It is highly likely that she left the country, and she might even be living off the grid. When he says that, I picture her in a long sundress and wide brimmed sun hat and sunglasses, walking the beach of some exotic shores. Maybe she's found her paradise after all.

He goes on to say that he suspects she is likely with someone else, rather than being alone. That makes sense, and I also believe she is with someone. Mama could never exist alone. Silence and solitude drove her crazy; she couldn't be alone with her own thoughts. She needed to fill the days and nights with other people, so she wouldn't have to deal with her mind. You aren't going to get away with it Mama. I won't stop looking for you, and I will make you accountable for your actions. I am considering hiring a private detective. The police have many theories, but I need answers.

I'm not looking for another relationship, but I've been alone for awhile when I meet Jeep. His real name is Gavin Pierce, shortened to G.P., nicknamed Jeep. He's not a musician, which might actually be a good thing. In fact, he's a mechanic where I take my car in to be serviced. I appreciate not having to deal with music talk day in and day out. His schedule is regular, there's no touring to worry about, he wears work clothes instead of leather jackets. It is refreshing to be with someone who is not in the business.

Jeep adores me and treats me so well. He sends flowers to me at work. He writes love notes, and calls me cute nicknames. I enjoy the attention, it helps me to forget about my worries and regrets. We spend the first few months getting to know each other then he asks me about my family and wants to introduce me to his. I tell him who Daddy is, and he thinks that's pretty cool.

I don't mention that I haven't spoken to Daddy for several months, after I called to tell him that Eric and I had split up. Daddy was disappointed; we ended up butting heads over my life and my future. Again, he was trying to parent me when he has no right. He told me not to turn into Mama, and that's when I decided to put a bit of space between us. The last time he called, I didn't call him back. I will eventually, but it all just hurts so damn bad.

I tell Jeep the bare minimum about Mama. I don't bother to say she's missing. I don't want to get into that, that's my own business. I just tell him she lives far away and we are estranged; that's the truth of it anyway. I know that I'm keeping Jeep at arm's length when he's only been open and honest with me, but I don't get too close. I build walls, I maintain distance. I'm unable to throw myself into relationships, being exposed and vulnerable. It's not a conscious choice, it's just how it is. He often tells me that I seem to be a million miles away. He thinks I'm distracted, maybe thinking about work, but the truth of it is, I don't know how to get closer. I really like him, so it's beyond frustrating that I can't get past whatever it is that stops me from just living life without always having to be on guard.

In contrast to me, with hardly any family to speak of, Jeep has a huge family. He is one of five children, with countless in laws, nieces, nephews and cousins. He grew up in a large, close-knit nuclear family. I meet a lot of them at once for the first time when we attend a family barbecue at his parent's house. There are so many faces and names to remember; so many questions to field. They want to get to know me, but it's uncomfortable. I'm not used to this. My world has always been very insular, very private. Suddenly I'm surrounded by Jeep's family every time I turn around. They all live fairly close to each other, so they see each other often. Someone is always coming to visit. Someone is always popping in "just for a moment". There are countless family gatherings, birthdays, celebrations to attend. It's hard for me to adjust to being constantly bombarded by people and questions. I feel like they must be judging me, and I'm failing.

They are all wonderful people though, who welcome me with open arms. His mother and father are lovely people with humble blue-collar roots. They go out of their way to make me feel like a part of the family. They are so happy that Jeep has found someone. His brothers and sisters, two of each, are very friendly; they envelope me into their group, as if I'm one of them. They are all great. They are the perfect family. There's nothing wrong with them...but there's something wrong with me. I can't handle it.

I start to feel smothered, even annoyed. I'm not used of having so many people demanding my attention, asking questions about my life. I find it hard not to reveal too much about myself without looking rude or suspicious. I'm trying to balance all of them versus my love for Jeep. This is just a normal relationship, with normal expectations of a new partner, but I'm drowning. Trying to be normal makes me feel like I am drowning, how sad is that? Why can't I just be like other people? Why can't I just enjoy all these people and their embrace their offer of friendship and acceptance? I just end up being toxic to anyone who tries to love me.

After a few more months of trying to juggle all the balls in the air, I let them drop. I break Jeep's heart, just as I have broken Eric's and Jack's. I push him away, but I don't want to. I end up breaking my own heart also.

I try dating a couple more people after Jeep. There are nothing wrong with these men or their families either, but the same thing happens, I freak out and push them away. I cannot control the overwhelming urge to run, the urge to keep people at a distance. I'm afraid to let them see me for who I am. I don't want them to find out about my life and the way I grew up, and reject me for it. It hurts that my childhood has screwed me up so badly, that I can't accept the love of perfectly good people. I'm so messed up. I'm angry at myself. I'm angry at the world.

II:

I have no one else to talk to, so I finally relent and call Daddy. I need someone to hear me. I try telling him how angry I am, how it's affecting my life and my ability to connect to people. The only thing he contributes is to suggest that I find someone to talk to about it. The thought of talking to a stranger about my life is revolting. I just wanted some words of wisdom, something to ease my mind, someone to tell me that I'm not crazy. I don't need to be told to go to a shrink. He's also still pressuring me to come and meet his new family. I can't talk to him anymore right now.

My loneliness and restless anger causes me to do something long overdue, and I surprise myself with own my bravery. Many years have passed, but I need to know why Uncle Freddie didn't keep his promise. He said he would find me. That was the last thing I heard on my way out the door, and I held onto that hope for a long time, until Stark's fists started flying. That's why I finally gave up, I was utterly defeated and felt all alone in the world. It was one of the lowest moments in my life. In contrast, living with Uncle Freddie was a bright light in my tumultuous childhood. I have many good memories of that time, and I mourn for the loss of that family. I also mourn for that little girl who finally found love, only to have it cruelly yanked away. I need to understand what happened back then, so I can let go of the pain and anger.

I sit at my kitchen table, thinking and staring at the phone. After some hesitation, I figure I have nothing to lose. Finding the number easily in the phone book, I dial quickly, before I change my mind. I get an answering machine.

"Uncle Freddie, this is Sunni. I know it's been a long time but I just want you to know that I'm okay. I miss you all and I'm hoping you'll call me back. I need to talk..."

There's a loud click and a beep, and his anxious voice comes on the line, "Hello? Hello, Sunni?"

His familiar voice makes me smile. We spend a lot of time catching up before we talk about anything serious. I talk to Kate and thank her for being my mother when I needed one, and to let the girls know how great it was to have sisters, even for a little while. Talking to Kate warms my heart and brings back a flood of good memories. Being able to thank her for selflessly keeping me after Mama ran off, and treating me as one of her own, is something I've always wanted to do. No one else ever did anything for me when I was growing up. My life would have turned out so differently if only I was able to stay, if only everyone cared as much as they did. Kate begins to apologize for losing me, but I stop her. It's not her fault; the fault lies solely with Mama, and I don't want her to carry that guilt. Kate is crying when she hands the phone back to Uncle Freddie.

He tells me that they thought about me, worried about me, every day. His voice fills with emotion when I tell him I waited for them to come and rescue me for a long time before I gave up. They had called the police right away, they spent many sleepless nights worrying themselves sick that I might be in danger. They felt helpless, and even drove around looking themselves when the police came up empty handed. Mama kept me hidden so well that I couldn't be found. After spending months in turmoil, they finally had to accept the fact that I wouldn't be coming back. They had to let go to save their own world, so it didn't destroy their family. He assures me that I was never, ever forgotten. After hanging up with Uncle Freddie, I'm overwhelmed with peace. Seeing the situation through his eyes makes me feel better. I can only hope that all the information I provided to the detective will result in justice for us someday. It's sad that Mama trampled through many lives, destroying each one with her selfish actions.

III:

I'm going through the motions of a life. The routine of work is monotonous, but necessary. I do find some peace of mind losing myself in the music, but I'm struggling. I wonder if packing up and moving will help, but there's nowhere for me to go. I curse Mama for the legacy that she has left me. I'm so mad at her. I try writing her letters that I can never send just to get it all out of my head, but when I try to put my feelings onto paper, I just get frustrated and crumple it up and throw it across the room. A lifetime of resentment and fury are destroying me slowly from the inside out. I'm drowning, I'm smothering, and I don't know how to save myself.

This is the mind set I'm in when I meet Steve. He is a drummer in a well established heavy metal band, that I meet when I'm assisting with production of their latest album. He's easily a foot taller than me, stocky, but muscular, reminding me of a football player. His head is shaved, and he has a goatee. He asks me out after our work together is finished. I have nothing to lose, no expectations, and even lower standards. I don't really care anymore. I'm at the lowest point of my life.

Steve is different than any of the other men that have been in my life. He is gruff, and rough around the edges. He's quiet and reserved; and he's angry at the universe like me. We've both had rough lives and I feel that he understands me. Steve was in foster homes for much of his life due to an abusive, alcoholic father and an unfit mother. He understands what it's like to grow up with dysfunction. We bond over our similarities, and share our stories. I'm able to tell my truth without judgment, because he gets it, and he often has an even worse story to tell me. We each understand what the other has been through. With Steve, I don't have to pretend to be happy or pretend that I'm okay.

Our relationship starts out slow. We go for coffee a few times, we go out to dinner. Things are going well, despite the fact that he tends to lose patience easily and he's quick to anger over little things. He's calm with me, but I notice the brief flicker of anger in his eyes when dealing with situations and people like slow waiters, bad drivers, and other common irritations. He also has no patience for fans that recognize him in public; he brushes them off, often rudely, and refuses to sign autographs. The paparazzi that find us and take pictures of us anger him and he will lash out at them and break their cameras. We end up the fodder for entertainment news magazines detailing his crazy public behaviour. Despite all this, I appreciate the fact that he's authoritative and serious. His strong personality is completely different than what I'm used to. It doesn't feel like I'm dating a carbon copy of Eric anymore.

As Steve becomes more comfortable with me, as we get to know each other better, his true colours begin to show. His temper rears it's ugly head every day. The first time he really directs his anger at me is several months into the relationship when he wants to move in with me. He's over at my place a lot and thinks we might as well just save money and live together. I'm not ready to give up my freedom yet. I'm still hurting from Eric and Jeep and Jack and Michael and Mama and Daddy, and a million other things. When I tell Steve no, I'm not ready for that step yet, he slams his fist down on the table, his face turning red. Instead of running for the hills right then and there, I ignore all the red flags, and instantly revert back to childhood where the little voice in my head tells me to behave, be good, be quiet...someone is angry and I'm 8 years old again.

Steve moves in and he takes over my entire life. He wastes no time; he becomes controlling and sets down rules. He drops me off at work and picks me up. He gets angry when I want to call Daddy, so I don't. He yells, he demands, he orders, he isolates me, and I let him do it all. I justify it all because he never lays a hand on me. He never hits me. I'm in too deep, and my apathy won't let me get out. I feel like I deserve this, and I let the universe punish me - for hurting Jack, Eric and Jeep, for being a burden that Mama had to bear, for being born...

When he's in a good mood, we are fine, but his dark moods come on without warning. I'm walking around on egg shells more often than not. His behaviour escalates over the following months. Now he shoves, pulls hair - eventually he starts twisting my arm behind my back and pushing me into the wall, snarling angrily in my ear. Still, he never hits me. Steve is so much like Stark and Michael, and I am now following Mama's path a little too closely. Even that realization doesn't wake me up.

I haven't spoken to Daddy in months, even though he's called me several times. I'm sure he's seen the stories about Steve in the music news. The media has managed to confirm that I am indeed his daughter, but thankfully they don't dig into it any farther than that. Headlines are screaming "Graham Sage's Daughter in Relationship with Volatile Drummer", with accompanying pictures of us in dark glasses, trying to shield our faces from the cameras; Steve with his perpetual scowl on his face. I'm sure Daddy's calling to try and warn me, trying to make me see what's right in front of my face. I don't return his calls. How can I explain the life I'm living now? He'll think I'm a fool; he won't approve. I can't deal with anymore judgment. I hear on the radio that he has gone back on the road, playing shows in several big cities across the country. He was supposed to take an extended break, possibly retire, but he can't stay away from the music. Eric, on the other hand, is finished his cross country tour. When I see him on the tv entertainment news program, it tugs at my heart, so I turn it off. I don't want to know anymore.

IV:

Only when I almost die, do I finally come back to my senses and see my life for what it has become. It is after midnight, late summer. It has been particularly hot all week. The windows are open, and a fan blows hot air around the apartment. We are watching tv in bed, I'm falling asleep. I wake up to Steve kissing my neck. I'm hot, I'm tired, I just want to be left alone. I push him away and roll over.

It is impossible for me to know everything that happens next, because it all happens so fast. He immediately reacts to the rejection by yelling that I have some nerve. I roll back over and I'm met with a backhand to the face. I touch my cheek and wince. He's never hit me before, but of course it was inevitable. Of course it was. It was just a matter of time, and I knew that, and I ignored it.

He's yelling and he's hitting and punching, and I struggle to get out of the bed but he's on top of me. He's out of control and I'm fighting for my life. I try to get my foot up to push him off, but he catches my toes in his hand and bends them backwards purposely until I feel two of them crack. His face is contorted, and I don't recognize him with the mask of anger he wears. I'm screaming now, trying to punch him in the face. I connect with his nose, and it allows me to flip over onto my stomach and scramble off the bed. When I set foot on the floor, my injured toes touch down first and I fall in pain. I'm crawling across the floor trying to get out of the bedroom, out of the house. He grabs me from behind and flips me onto my back, ripping at my nightshirt. The last thing I remember is his hands around my neck choking me as he bashes the back of my head into the floor over and over again.

I open my eyes briefly. There are lights above my head and I'm moving, people are staring down at me yelling back and forth amongst each other; someone is trying to talk to me. I'm being rolled down the hospital hallway on a stretcher. There is chaos around me. I let my eyes close.

I struggle to pull myself out of the heavy darkness and open my eyes. I'm laying in a hospital bed, hooked up to machines, there's a mask over my face. Nurses come over to my beside. I think I see Daddy in the corner of the room, but I must be imagining things. I'm so tired. I fade away.

I hear a low steady beeping and people talking in hushed tones. Then I feel the pain; my whole body screams in agony. My eyes flutter, trying to open but everything is blurry and the harsh lights hurt. I groan. I look around. A doctor comes to my bedside and Daddy follows him over, a stricken look on his face.   ----

V:

The neighbours heard all the noise and called the police. I'm told that I have been in and out of consciousness for a few days. When I wake up, Daddy is by my side. The hospital called him, as my next of kin and he flew in immediately, cutting his tour short. My memory is murky, but they gently tell me what happened. I'm embarrassed...ashamed. Steve fled before the police arrived, and he still hasn't been found. Everyone always runs. I want to run too, and hide from all of it, but I can't even sit up by myself. My injuries are explained to me bluntly; I'm lucky to be alive. There is some possibility that I might never be able to have children due to the severity of the sexual assault. Multiple broken ribs from being kicked, numerous stitches in my head, a lacerated spleen which had to be removed, broken fingers and toes from fighting so hard, and bruising all over – this is what he left me with. It will be a long, slow recovery.

It is in this moment that I miss Mama more than I ever have before. I don't know why. I'm an emotional and physical wreck. Pain medications keep putting me to sleep. I feel stupid and sorry for myself. I'm overwhelmingly sad, but I don't cry. There are no tears, even now, only when the pain in my body becomes unbearable.

I get a lot of flowers; new ones seem to come every day. My room is filled with bright colours and sweet smells. There are flowers from people at work, people I used to work with at home, other people I have met in the music business. I even receive flowers from Jack, and even more surprisingly, from Kip. Word of the attack seems to have spread quickly around the music world, and thanks to Steve's fame, the media as well. I'm horrified that all these people know and I'm afraid of what they might think of me. Daddy says not to be silly, it just means a lot of people care about me. He says I should feel blessed, not embarrassed.

People have been calling the hospital to ask about me. The media has reached out, wanting a statement, wanting to know when I will be available for an interview. I don't return their calls. I don't want to talk to anyone, but Daddy tries to field some of them for me, telling them thank you for their concern, but I am not well right now and I need time and space. We appreciate your privacy at this time – the typical reply to the media when anything goes wrong. The media runs stories anyway, despite not having any real idea of what happened. This is breaking news and they follow along closely. Daddy has been spotted going in and out of the hospital, adding a whole new level of exposure to my story. Reporters try to get him to say something, to give them any information at all, but he only says, "No comment", as he walks past them. Whatever details they don't know, they seem to make up. It all just makes me retreat even further into myself.

Daddy is staying at a motel nearby and spends every day with me at the hospital. We talk and we grow close. He apologizes over and over again, but it's not his fault, not directly anyway. The police visit multiple times to ask me questions. They say Steve will face jail time because he has prior assault convictions. They also tell me that they will find him. I might have to testify and that terrifies me.

Healing is slow, so much damage has been done, not only physically but mentally. The thought that I might never be able to have children makes me sad, even if I'm not sure that I'd ever want any. It's just one more thing that's possibly been stolen from me in my life. The doctor suggests that I might want to talk to someone to help me get through it all. I refuse vehemently. I own my life story and I choose who to share it with. I have no desire to talk to anyone, let alone a stranger. My Pandora's box of traumas remains locked.

On a dark fall evening, long after Daddy leaves for the night, I'm laying in the bed uncomfortable and in pain, but pain meds are not due for awhile. I fidget and try to make myself comfortable. There's a shadow in my doorway and I look up and gasp.

"Eric...." my voice is a whisper.

He's standing there awkwardly, looking unsure of himself.

I motion him into the room and hold out my arms. I didn't realize how badly I need him, how badly I miss him. He comes towards me and gingerly gives me a gentle hug; his familiar embrace feels so good. There are tears in his eyes when he sees me and all my injuries. My face is bruised and swollen. It's only been a week since the attack.

"How did you know..." There's a catch in my voice and a lump in my throat.

"Graham called me. He wasn't sure if he should, if you'd be mad, but he did anyway. I drove up as soon as I heard. Aww Sunni, why..." he leaves his sentence unfinished and looks away.

"I don't know...I just..." I don't know what to say.

"I've missed you." He says, and looks back at me...and that's when the dam bursts. The tears fall like they've never fallen before. I sob uncontrollably, gasping, unable to catch my breath. He sits on the bed beside me and holds me. He doesn't say anything, he just lets me cry. I can finally let all my defenses down, and stop pretending to be strong. He knows me, he's the only one that really knows me. It's alright now, I can just let it all out. It's been a long time since we broke up, but it's like we were never apart.

We talk well past when visiting hours are over. I apologize over and over again for leaving him. I tell him that I thought I was doing the right thing, but since then, everything's been wrong. I apologize for being screwed up. I start to babble, trying to explain and justify my actions; my words becoming incoherent through my sobs. He shushes me and calms me - he always did have the ability to centre me. He understands why I left, but had a hard time dealing with the fact that he couldn't convince me to stay. Thinking he wasn't good enough or that he failed, sent him into a depression, even though he knew the issues were mine. We talk through all of it, things are better, but the guilt will always remain. I hurt him deeply, but he's willing to forgive me, even though I won't forgive myself. When Daddy comes back the next morning, he's afraid I'm mad at him, but I give him a big hug and whisper, "Thank you," in his ear.

Eric stays by my side through all of it. Daddy stays too. For the first time in such a long time, I feel like I'm not alone. They sit with me for hours on end; they comfort me when the nightmares wake me up with a start. They let me cry, talk or be silent; whatever I need and they don't ever judge, question or shame me. I'm in the hospital for almost a month before I'm well enough to be discharged, and they've both been there the whole time.

The week before I leave the hospital, the police make one last visit to tell me that Steve has been found and arrested. He's being held in custody for a bail hearing. If he pleads guilty, there will be no trial, but if he makes any other plea or there are any other unforeseen circumstances, I will need to go to court. I have already given police my official statement and answered numerous, repetitive and embarrassing questions. It's all too much to deal with. The thought of facing him in court sends me into a panic attack. I'm given a sedative to calm me down and it puts me to sleep. I wish I could just sleep through all of it and wake up when the nightmare is over. But this nightmare hasn't stopped since I was born.

VI:

I don't feel safe here. I can't live in this city anymore. There are no good memories and nothing keeping me here. When I get out of the hospital, Eric arranges to have my apartment packed up and moved back home. I don't even want to set foot in it and he doesn't let me. He also arranges to have it cleaned because I'm not wiping my own blood off the floor.

The police say that I can certainly leave the city and go home, I will just have to return if there is a trial, but I can't think about that now. I just need to get out of here. I quit my job without a second thought. My inclination right now is to quit the music business entirely – just run from all the people who know what happened to me. Daddy says this is just a knee-jerk reaction, and if I give it some time, I will change my mind. Eric says he knows I love music and songwriting so much that he doesn't even believe me. I guess we'll all find out.

Daddy travels back home with us and Eric moves me right in with him. My stuff follows days later but I end up storing or selling most of it. I can't handle any reminders. Daddy stays with us a few extra days and then he says, if I'm well enough, he should be going home. Now that he knows I will be alright and will be taken care of, his mind is at ease. I can't thank him enough for what's he done just by being there for me and making me feel like I matter to him. When we see him off at the airport, I know I will see him again. It is not an emotional, melancholy goodbye like the first time.

I spend the next days resting, sleeping, healing. Sitting in a chair with a cup of coffee looking out at the ocean churning settles my mind and calms my nerves. I spend a lot of time just watching the waves and contemplating my life. Sometimes Eric sits with me quietly. We don't try to talk over the roar of the water, we just sit together. He holds my hand and I let him. We are making our way back to each other slowly. I'm sure he's afraid to trust me given my history of bolting, so I will have to prove it to him if I want to have any credence with him. I'm still afraid those feelings of needing to run might come back, so I don't even know if I'm trustworthy yet.

I have developed what I'm sure is some post traumatic stress – nightmares and panic attacks triggered by the littlest things or nothing at all. Eric urges me to go to a doctor and get a diagnosis, but he doesn't push. He knows I will just do what I see fit. He doesn't challenge my stubbornness. Often, I'm afraid to go to sleep at night because I know it is almost certain that I will wake up in a cold sweat, crying or yelling for help. Eric wakes up with me and calms me down in his quiet way every time. He tells me it's alright, I'm okay, it's over now. He stays up with me for as long as I'm awake, not closing his own eyes until I'm sleeping. He's infinitely patient with the disruptions to his own sleep, his own life. I apologize a lot, but he assures me in no certain terms that this is how he wants it. He wants to take care of me, and I don't push him away this time.

When I'm fully awake and the bad dreams have faded, we lay there in the dark and talk in low whispers, like we used to do all those years ago. It seems like a million years have passed since those days. I've lived a million lifetimes since then. I'm trying to open my Pandora's box to him. I begin, little by little, to reveal all the things I've never told him before, all the things I haven't even written here – things that I have pushed so far out of my mind that I lose my breath whenever I try to recall them. It hurts so badly to say the words out loud, to share things I've never wanted anyone to know. Eric never judges, he never reacts, no matter what I tell him. He just loves and accepts me anyway. He is the best therapist without even knowing it, I don't need anyone else to talk to. My heart aches for the little girl who was hurt and lonely and scared all the time. Everyone failed her; no one saved her. How did she even live through it all? I realize now how strong she was – how strong I was - and how strong I am.

There is no point in checking in with Detective Killian, but I call just to let him know I'm back in town, hopefully for good, but who knows what the future might hold. He assures me that he will call if there's ever any information to share about Mama. I leave it in his hands. Mama has been gone for a long time now. I can't believe she would outright abandon me for good, but on the other hand, I'm surprised she took so long to do it. If she did this disappearing act when I was younger, my life might have been so different. What do I know, maybe it would have turned out exactly the same regardless – how much control do I really have in my own life anyway? Right now, absolutely none.

The police contact me to talk to me about Steve. Just hearing his name causes my heart to pound. They tell me that bail was denied and he will remain in custody. That fills me with relief, as I keep having a dream that he would get bail, go on the run and come looking for me. In my dream, he teams up with Stark and they both hunt me down and kill me. My relief is short lived however, when I am informed that the matter will be going to trial. The Prosecutor and the Defense are unable to reach a plea deal. Steve wants to plead not guilty; his lawyer wants to use a mental illness defense, to get him psychiatric help instead of jail time. Prosecutors want him in prison. I will have to come back and testify. Without me, he may get off with time served or be able to get a much lesser charge. They say the prosecuting attorney will be contacting me to discuss the details. So until then, I wait. I just want it all to go away, but I won't be able to run away from this, the only way is through.

Word has gotten around that I'm back in town. People are calling Eric trying to reach me. They ask to talk to me, but I have no desire to talk to anyone. I ask Eric to tell them nothing, so all he says is that I'm doing well, thank you for your concern. I know they likely mean well, and I love my music community, but right now I don't trust anyone. I might never trust anyone ever again. I just feel like I'm in limbo right now; my life is on pause. I don't know what my future holds. I might not even go back to the music business. I have been mulling this option over in my head. I know this would be running away instead of confronting my demons, but that seems to be the only thing I know how to do; the only thing my Mama ever taught me.

Jack has called Eric a few times since I've been back home to check on me. He's spoken to Eric, but I haven't wanted to talk. He and Eric remain good friends. They have no hard feelings towards each other because of me. Unexpectedly, Jack appears at Eric's one evening. I'm resting in bed when Eric comes to tell me that Jack is here and would like to see for himself that I'm alright. My first inclination is to refuse, but I surprise myself by agreeing to see him. I follow Eric out of the bedroom and Jack is standing in the living room looking out the window. He looks exactly the same as I left him. Seeing him brings back all sorts of memories, most of them good, of life on the road, of the excitement of being new to the business, of long lost love. He turns towards me, smiles and walks over to give me a big hug. I hug him back, it's like reuniting with a ghost from the past.

We sit in the living room and Jack sits beside me holding my hands in his. Eric offers to leave us alone to talk, but we both insist that he stays. There is no more love left between us, but there is also no anger. It's all water under the bridge, and it's just nice to see an old friend. Jack says he's glad I'm feeling better and he's sorry for what happened to me. He's going to make me cry, so I change the subject and ask him about his life. He tells me he's a solo artist now – the band never did recover from that first and only tour. They kept it together for awhile afterwards, but there was too much in-fighting to even accomplish another album, so they split up and pursued their own careers. Jack has just released his first solo album, and is leaving on tour to promote it soon. He says he needed to see me before he left so he knew I was going to be alright. We talk about the good times and share some laughs. Jack tells Eric to take good care of me, and by the time he leaves, I feel a sense of closure that I didn't get by leaving the tour all of those years ago.

This is exactly the feeling of peace that I hope to achieve for myself by confronting Mama. I need to heal the open wounds that life with her has left me with; raw, open wounds that continue to affect my life. I need to put a stop to the dysfunction so it does not continue to follow me any longer, stealing more of my life. I don't want to live like this anymore. I don't want to hurt anymore, and I don't want to hurt anyone else. As soon as this business with Steve is over, I have decided I will hire a private detective and focus all my efforts on finding her.

VII:

The day I am dreading arrives in early fall. I have been communicating with the Prosecutor, preparing for court, and now it is time to fly back to the city and deal with Steve. I am terrified, but I don't have the option of hiding my head in the sand, I need to do this. I don't feel strong right now, but I have the support of Daddy and Eric, and that will get me through. Daddy offers to come with us, to be there in person for me, but I say no. I don't want to look over and see his face during the trial, looking at me with despair. I don't want him present to hear all the sordid details that might come out.

When we arrive in the city, Eric and I take a motel room and go to meet with the Prosecutor at the court house. Mr Falconi is a tall and imposing man, dressed neatly in a grey suit and matching tie. He shakes my hand warmly and thanks me for coming, saying that not only will my testimony ensure that

Steve goes to jail, but will save another woman from suffering what I did. He explains the process, what is going to happen, where everyone is going to sit and their roles. When he points to where Steve will be sitting, it triggers panic. The thought of seeing Steve in person in the courtroom makes me feel physically ill. Mr Falconi tells me not to look at Steve, just focus on him while I am on the stand. He warns me that the Defense will do everything they can in Steve's interests, so to be prepared to hear some things that I might not like.

A couple days later, Eric and I sit in the hallway of the courtroom. I'm shaky and nauseous, and try to calm myself by taking deep breaths. There were several reporters camped outside that were taking pictures and yelling questions as we walked in. The media is selling stories and making money off of my trauma – what a strange, sad world we live in. I keep my head down and walk on past despite their pleas for a comment, with Eric shielding me the best he can from their prying cameras and microphones. I won't read the stories they write about me – it's all tabloid garbage, and half of it will likely be lies. I have chosen not to sit in on the whole trial, so I am just waiting to be called in. I have the right to attend all of it, but I don't think I can handle it. I don't want to be in a room with Steve that long. It is hard enough to re-live everything.

Eric is holding my hand tightly, with his arm around me, when they come into the hall and call my name. I stand up and feel faint. I take a moment to steady myself and Eric nods at me encouragingly, and whispers, "You got this," with a smile. I nod at him, looking way more confident than I actually feel and walk forward. The bailiff opens the wooden double doors and steps aside for me. Every face in the courtroom is looking back at me, but I have developed tunnel vision. I focus on the seat I will be sitting in and head straight for it, not looking left or right. Eric takes a seat at the back of the audience near the door. I look up nervously at the judge, and he acknowledges me with a nod. Even though I was trying to avoid doing so, I feel compelled to look over at the Defense table. I see Steve staring daggers at me; his face is contorted in anger, taking me right back to that night. It takes me a moment to compose myself. My hands are shaking, but they are clutched together tightly on my lap where no one can see. I feel like I can't breathe, and an uncomfortable warmth floods over me, making me feel nauseous and faint, but I won't let Steve see me looking afraid. I won't give him the satisfaction. I need to summon all the strength in the world right now to get through this. It will take everything I have, but if there's one thing I'm used to, it's getting myself through difficult circumstances. I harden my eyes and hold his gaze; he can't hurt me here. He needs to pay for what he's done. I can't make anyone else pay for the things I've suffered, but I can make him pay.

It's hard to talk about my relationship with Steve knowing that Eric is listening, as well as the media who will be publishing the outcome as soon as they hear it. I answer all of Mr Falconi's questions, some very personal – it's very difficult to make the words come out of my mouth, but I do it. He starts out simple, asking me about myself, when and why I moved to city, what I do for a living. He transitions into how and when I met Steve, what our relationship was like in the beginning, and when things started to change. I readily admit to ignoring all the red flags about Steve until it was too late. We get to the hard part. He details my injuries to the court, shows pictures taken by the police – I look away, and glance at Eric. He looks horrified...devastated. I've hurt him by letting someone hurt me.

Steve is leaning back in his chair with a smirk on his face - he looks almost proud. He leans in and whispers something to his lawyer and they share a slight laugh. That's when it happens. That's when my fear turns into anger. I'm ready to end this. I force the shakiness out of the my voice, and somehow I find a strength that has always been there when I've needed it. I will not let this pitiful man intimidate me. I am not 8 years old anymore. At the end of the day, only one of us will be walking out of here, and I will be forgetting him and leaving his memory in the past.

I tell my truth and I don't mince words. I may not remember everything that happened after I was knocked out, but I do remember enough. I field the Defense Attorney's questions. I can tell that Steve doesn't have a leg to stand on. They are grasping at straws. It is my turn to smirk now, and I look Steve right in the eye and do just that, making sure he sees me. I will not be ashamed to tell the court exactly what he did to me because none of this is my fault. I will also no longer be ashamed of anything that happened during my time with Mama, none of that is my fault either.

When my testimony is over, I step off the stand, my head held high. I have no doubt that there will be more nightmares, there will be more tears, but I won't be held hostage by any of it anymore. I'm taking control. I have never had any control in my whole life, but I have made the decision to have it now. I don't even look at Steve as I walk right past his table. He is nothing, he is just a regret from my past. I've made peace with this part of my life. Now all I need to do is look Mama in the eye, and have my peace with her. For the first time, I am hopeful. I may have walked into the court house with my head hanging, but I walk out with it held high. I'm proud of myself for surviving this whole ordeal, and I realize that I should be proud for surviving all along.

We stay in the city for the rest of the week, until the trial is over, in case I need to be called back to the stand. Steve is convicted of charges of second degree sexual battery and aggravated assault, and because he did not accept the Prosecutor's original plea deal, he will be going back to jail. Sentencing will be held at another time, but I won't be back to find out. I'm washing my hands of this whole thing and walking away.

VIII:

On the way home, I'm feeling good. Eric and I have a lot to talk about, but we don't talk about the trial. We will never mention Steve's name again. I thank him for being there for me, for being who he is, for loving me despite everything. He doesn't say anything, but he looks over at me while he's driving, grins and squeezes my hand. We don't know what the future is going to hold for us, whether we will be together or not, where life might take us from here, but right now in this moment, we are good. A huge weight has been lifted off my shoulders, and for the first time in a long time, I feel like I can breathe. I have put a lot of the bad stuff behind me, and I'm looking forward to working on the rest. Eric is proud of me. I am too. I can't wait to get home and focus all my efforts of finding Mama. Eric agrees to help me get a private detective.

He knows how important, how necessary, this is for me.

I am tired when we arrive back home. The emotional weight of the previous days hits me all at once, and all I want to do is take a hot bath and go to sleep. The answering machine is flashing with messages, and Eric is checking them, as I close the bathroom door and turn on the water.

Before I can get in the tub, Eric is knocking on the door. He tells me that I have a message from Detective Killian on the phone and I better call him back.

2001-2002: The Tragic Years

I:

Mama's body was pulled from the river on the outskirts of town. Her car was also found in the water nearby. We are at the police station and Detective Killian is telling me all the details, but I can't hear anything else he's saying. As soon as I hear that she is dead it hits me like a ton of bricks, and I feel absolutely gutted. I fall to the floor on my knees, my mouth open in a scream, but nothing comes out because I can't breath. Tears stream down my face and I'm choking...and I feel like I'm dying.

Eric pulls me up onto a chair, and he's holding onto me tight. I'm shaking and my head is spinning – I feel like I'm going to pass out. Detective Killian hands me tissues and says he is sorry for my loss, but he has no idea what I have lost. I have lost a mother; an unfit, neglectful, selfish mother who took me with her on a journey of craziness and pain. The mother who stole my childhood, destroyed my relationship with Daddy, and left me with issues I'm only now beginning to understand. All my coping mechanisms, bad relationships, personality flaws and failings are all her fault. She gifted me with the inability to know myself and the inability to trust. She left me alone over and over again, so that I learned the pain of abandonment so completely and thoroughly that I ended up abandoning others. She taught me everything not to do as a mother and as a human being. Despite all the anger I hold for this woman, she was still the only mother I ever knew. My heart aches for her and aches for myself. I wanted to confront her so badly, to bring her to her senses – but then after that confrontation I wanted to get to know her as an adult, to understand her, so that we could develop a new relationship. So maybe, just maybe, I could experience her love. Now I won't ever have that opportunity. I won't ever have closure. I will forever be a motherless child.

When I gain control of my senses and am able to listen to Detective Killian again, he goes on to tell me that the coroner estimates that Mama has been in the water for a very long time. They have determined she likely died very soon after she disappeared for the final time. She never left town. In fact, she was close by this whole time. She didn't leave me to go live the good life somewhere far away; she didn't forget about me. She didn't want to disappear for good, and she didn't kill herself. It is unbelievable to think that she has been dead all this time and I never knew, I never felt it. I don't know why I would expect to. There was never a connection in life, so why would there be in death, but I can't help feeling that I should have known.

These details cause a new tidal wave of tears. All the anger I harboured towards Mama for disappearing and never coming back was all wrong. I have carried that anger as a badge of honor for so long, and all this time, I was angry at her for something that wasn't her fault. I assumed the worst, but why wouldn't I? She didn't intend to leave me. She would have come back if she could have. Our story could have ended differently, but we were both robbed when she died.

Before he tells me how she died, Detective Killian wants to know if I can handle more information right now, or do I need a moment. I tell him just to please tell me everything all at once, because I need to be devastated only one time. I cannot go through this a second time. He takes a deep breath and tells me that Mama was murdered. She had been shot in the back of the head and thrown in the water. I didn't think my heart could hurt anymore than it does, but I gasp in shock and murmur, "Oh no... no...no...", and shake my head. Eric's grip on me tightens, and if he wasn't holding onto me, I think I would fall over.

Detective Killian goes on to say that they were able to find her body because someone finally came forward with the missing piece of the puzzle that they needed to solve her disappearance. Even though they had spoken to everyone at the beginning of the investigation, some people were too afraid to say anything. I interrupt him.

"It was Michael wasn't it? Buddy's friend? I know it was him. He hurt me too. She ran away to get away from him and he followed her and killed her..." I'm rambling, my words coming out in a tumble of emotion.

The detective holds up his hand and I stop talking.

"No Sunni. We thoroughly investigated both Michael and Buddy. They were our first suspects and we cleared both of them right at the beginning. Neither one of them had anything to do with this."

I don't respond. I look away. I know what's coming.

Detective Killian says the words that I'm expecting to hear, but it's still just as gut-wrenching.

"Stark killed your mother."

Shawn Wilder aka Stark, one of my worst childhood boogeymen hunted down and killed Annie Ducayne, my Mama. The man responsible for many a late night bad dream, who terrorized me and beat up Mama, had finished the job he would have inevitably done anyway, given enough time. I knew they would not let her get away with stealing their money to fund her escape, let alone leave her go knowing all their crimes and secrets.

It took Stark and his grunt Krane awhile to find her because we kept moving all over. A lot of time had passed, but it didn't matter to them. They were on a mission to even the score and get rid of any evidence against them. More importantly, he would teach her a lesson for leaving him. If I had been with her when they finally found her, they would have killed both of us. They had been prepared to kill both mother and child. They debated coming after me after they killed her, but decided it was too risky, and that I must have been too young at the time to know much. I would have been killed too – this fact floors me. Mama's abandonment ultimately ended up saving my life. She left me alone yet one more time, and that is the time she died...and I lived.

I ask the detective how they know all this; I want to know who talked to them. He tells me that Tru, the only person that was nice to me, that was actually a decent human being, in Stark's godforsaken compound, had reached out to him long after he first talked to her.

Not that the knowledge of what she knew wasn't eating her up inside, but Tru's reason for turning on Stark was not altogether altruistic. Stark had also killed her boyfriend a few years after we left, and eventually he threatened her life also. She didn't feel safe anymore, and since she couldn't leave the compound without suffering the safe fate as Mama, she reached out to law enforcement to protect her and put away Stark. I'm angry that she kept her secrets for so long, letting me worry and seethe. Not only I was already struggling with my feelings for a woman who had already deeply failed me as a mother, but because Tru chose to keep quiet for so long, I was also forced to believe that she threw me away for good. After all that I gave of myself to her, all that I lost because of her, I believed she had tossed me aside. My sacrifice and suffering meant nothing. For a long time I held on to the belief that she must have loved me in some way to keep me with her all that time, she must have needed me...but once she seemed to have left for good without any regard for me, it felt like she mustn't have loved me at all. That hurt. Of course, I know Stark is the one who actually physically took my mother away, but I'm almost more angry at Tru. I liked her. I expected more from her. She ended up being just one more person who disappointed me.

After Tru gave up Stark, the police raided the compound. They had no advance warning, so all the evidence of their crimes, and all the drugs and weapons, were in plain view. They took him in, and in interrogation, he implicated Krane.

Stark's gang was linked to many other crimes and a couple other unsolved murders. They are giving police a lot of information in a bid to save themselves from the death penalty. They will likely die a snitch's death in prison at some point. Most importantly, they will never be able to hurt anyone else, and I won't have to live my life looking over my shoulder like Mama did. And Mama, in a way, she was responsible for taking down the whole thing – but she paid the ultimate price. After destroying so much of my life, she ended up saving it.

II:

Detective Killian assures me that Stark will not be getting out of jail. He says he's sorry for my loss and that Mama's case did not have a better outcome. I thank him for all his work, and ask him if he's going to need anything from me. I am relieved when he says no. They have plenty of evidence, witnesses and they have confessions; and I have already given him a statement. He tells me that he will let me know when the trial is, if I want to attend to represent and honour my mother, but I don't know if I will. Maybe I'll feel differently when the time comes, but right now I can't imagine being there. I will honour Mama my own way, in my own time.

The next day, when Eric is gone to the studio and I am all

alone, I call Daddy. He congratulates me on the outcome of Steve's trial, but he knows something else is wrong. I start to cry when I tell him about Mama. Believing that she had taken off to go live somewhere happily ever after was a much easier thought to hold on to to than the reality of what happened. Knowing that someone callously killed her and tossed her aside like garbage is devastating. Her death means the loss of the hope I had that I would see her again some day. I will also never be able to confront her about the past. Most importantly, we have lost the opportunity to be able to work through it all and create a new relationship. I have been mad at Mama for so long - rage that has been building and eating me alive - but I never wanted her to pay for her sins with her life. I'm left with so much guilt for being angry at her, for being unable to help her, for being unable to save her.

Even though I would have completely understood if he didn't, Daddy says he will be at the funeral. He says he's coming for me, to support me, and he wants to be there. I will be planning a small ceremony, just for us; there is no one else who would come. Mama had burnt all her bridges; she had no real friends, Grandma Louise had long since passed away, and even Uncle Freddie was not interested in coming when I told him. She was truly alone in the world. I'm hoping wherever she is now, she has finally found peace.

III:

Mama's ceremony is held in the same small church in town that she was baptized in as a child. She will be laid to rest in the adjacent cemetery, in a plot next to her mother. She would not approve I'm sure, but there is nowhere else for her to go. We have paid for a small headstone that has her name, date of birth, and month and year of death, as provided by Stark to the police. He couldn't remember the exact date, but was fairly certain of the month. Even in death, Mama is incomplete.

There are only four of us at the church for the ceremony, Daddy and Eric sitting on either side of me in the front row, each of them holding one of my hands. This is more difficult than I expected it to be. The pastor gives his sermon, preaching about life and death. He didn't know Mama, but that's alright, neither did any of us, not really anyway. As he concludes, he asks if anyone would like to say anything on Mama's behalf. Even thought I don't have to, I have prepared something that I want to read. It is more for me than anyone else. Daddy pats my arm as I get up and stand at the pulpit, and even though it's just us, I'm nervous. Eric nods encouragingly.

My voice is shaky, but I begin to speak.

"Annie Ducayne was a free spirit, who didn't play by any rules. She blazed her own trail and took me along with her on her journey. She wasn't always the best equipped with the skills or means needed to take care of both of us, but she always maintained a fierce independence and was never satisfied with sitting still. She suffered from her own traumas in life that shaped her into the person that she became. In many ways, she was still that little girl searching for something to make her feel whole again..."

I pause for a moment, to wipe my eyes and catch my breath, and then I continue.

"For better or for worse, she was my Mama, and I suppose she loved me in her own way...and I must love her in my own way...our relationship was complicated. All the times that she left, she always came back for me, but this last time she didn't. It was not her choice to leave me this way. She would have returned, and that brings me a small comfort. If I learned anything from her, it was resilience, independence, and the belief that I can take care of myself and survive anything that's thrown at me. So thank you Mama, for what you were able to give me, and I understand that you weren't able to give what you didn't have. I hope you have found what you were always searching for."

Daddy starts clapping quietly, looking at me with tears in his eyes. Eric nods and smiles. I turn and thank the Pastor for the service, and he smiles warmly.

We walk over to the little cemetery beside the church, and stand huddled together while the coffin is lowered into the ground. I place a bouquet of white roses on the lid. I don't cry, but there is a lump in my throat and a palpable sadness in the air. The finality of it all is sinking in. This is not the closure I was looking for. I would have never wished Mama's story ended this way; she didn't deserve this. Rest easy Mama, you can stop running now.

After the ceremony, Daddy, Eric and I go out for supper and we drink a toast to Mama.

Epilogue: The Triumphant Years

I stand on a small outcrop of rocks down at the ocean side; the waves lapping at my feet. Looking up to the sky, I close my eyes and feel the warm sun on my face. So much has happened since Mama was laid to rest five years ago. Everything is different. Everything changes. The only constant in life, is it's unpredictability.

I'm lost in my thoughts, but I'm soon distracted by giggling. I open my eyes and look back over my shoulder. Daddy is sitting in a lounge chair on the beach, wearing Bermuda shorts, a colourful Hawaiian shirt and a big sun hat; his bare toes buried in the sand. He has a big smile on his face, as he watches the babies playing in the water. Twins - my raven haired miracle babies - a boy and a girl, born on a bright and sunny morning almost three years ago. My son... mine and Eric's son...Elliot Eric.... we call him Eli. He has an impish grin like his father and is mischievous, loving and kind. Our daughter Randi Jade...we call her R.J. She has big doe eyes that can melt your heart, and she's as charming as she is headstrong. They are perfect.

I absent-mindedly twist my wedding ring and smile, as I watch Eric popping out of the water making the children laugh and squeal. Daddy is taking pictures of them. He points the camera at me and takes a picture. I smile and wave. This is my life and I'm happy, genuinely happy. I no longer have the urge to flee. I am not my Mama...I AM NOT my Mama! I want to stay right where I am and soak up every moment of this life. I want to be here for every day of these children's lives. The cycle of chaos stops me with me. My children will never know anything that is not loving, and consistent and stable. I will protect them like a ferocious mother bear, and never let anyone hurt them. Their Mama will not be an enigma, and they won't ever have to wonder if they are loved. They will never know the confusion of rejection, the pain of abandonment, or the sting of loneliness. When they were born I promised them they will always know how deeply they are cherished.

Daddy's family is coming out to join him at our house next week. I finally relented after the babies were born and flew out to visit Daddy. I wanted to show him the twins, and I decided to take a chance and meet Marie and her sons. It went better than I expected; we hit it off pretty good. She is actually a very nice person, and she treats Daddy well. They seem to really be in love. She is very accepting of me and my relationship with Daddy, and I'm developing a relationship with her also. Sometimes when you take a chance, venture outside of your comfort zone, things actually work out. No one was more surprised than me.

Eric is still on top of the world with his career. His band is extremely successful, and have won several music awards. Their new hit, a cover of 'Sunni, Honey' debuted at the top of the charts. At their upcoming show, Daddy is going to join them on stage to sing it with them. I can't wait to see that, because I will be joining them too. I've finally recorded that duet with Eric, the one that he's been wanting me to do for so long, and we're going to sing it together on stage. This is also out of my comfort zone, but if it worked once, I'm willing to try it again. As for me, I couldn't stay away from my beloved music after all, but I still stay in the background, songwriting for the most part. My songs are sung not only by my husband, but by other artists, and my ballads are lauded for being haunting and emotional. In every song, there is a little piece of my story. If my duet with Eric is well received, maybe I'll start singing some of my own songs. Maybe.

I visit Mama's grave as often as I can. I sit alone quietly talking to her and making peace with the past. And I forgive her. I forgive her for all of it, so I can move on. I mourn for both of us, for two little girls who were terribly hurt by people who were supposed to take care of them.

Daddy is playing peekaboo with Eli, who is looking at him skeptically. R.J., on the other hand, is laughing hysterically.

She reaches out and grabs Daddy's hat off his head and runs away giggling. Daddy jumps up, and he and Eli chase her down the beach. Eric looks over at me and grins.

It is a good life.

SUNNI HONEY

-by Graham Sage & The Night Winds

There's a girl waiting for me back home
Her green eyes sparkle in the sun
It's been a long time since I've seen her face
I just can't wait until this day is done

Then I'm going home, going home
To see my Sunni (honey)

Sunni, honey, the sky's not blue without you
Sunni, honey, the ocean's don't roar when you're not near
Sunni,honey, the birds don't sing and the sun doesn't shine
Sunni, honey, I'm sure glad you're mine

I've been away such a long time
On the road is the loneliest place to be
And then I think of her sweet little face
And I know she's waiting so patiently for me

It's time to go home, go home
To see my Sunni (honey)

Sunni, honey, the sky's not blue without you
Sunni, honey, the ocean's don't roar when you're not near
Sunni,honey, the birds don't sing and the sun doesn't shine
Sunni, honey, I'm sure glad you're mine

And when I get home, she won't be alone
And I don't ever want to leave her again

She'll come running free when she sees me
That little girl is heaven sent

chorus til fade